1065

SI

Y

278

WN

$3

LP 1

Hard Times and Arnie Smith

**Center Point
Large Print**

**This Large Print Book carries the
Seal of Approval of N.A.V.H.**

Hard Times and Arnie Smith

CLIFTON ADAMS

CENTER POINT PUBLISHING
THORNDIKE, MAINE

This Center Point Large Print edition
is published in the year 2009 by arrangement with
Golden West Literary Agency.

The text of this Large Print edition is unabridged.
In other aspects, this book may vary
from the original edition.
Printed in the United States of America.
Set in 16-point Times New Roman type.

ISBN: 978-1-60285-372-0

Library of Congress Cataloging-in-Publication Data

Adams, Clifton.
  Hard times & Arnie Smith / Clifton Adams.
      p. cm.
  ISBN 978-1-60285-372-0 (library binding : alk. paper)
  1. Large type books. I. Title. II. Title: Hard times and Arnie Smith.

PS3551.D34H295 2009
813'.54--dc22

2008039224

CHAPTER ONE

On that day in the springtime of 1892 the personal wealth of Arnie Smith consisted of one saddle, a pistol, the odds and ends in his war bag, and the clothes on his back. At various times he had owned riding horses of questionable soundness, but at the time he got the letter he was riding a company animal. 'Ninety-two was a year of panic and hard times. It was the rare cowhand who could afford a horse of his own.

But the letter changed all that. Or seemed too.

"Dear Mr. Smith . . ."

Arnie lingered fondly over that formal salutation. As well as he could recall it was the first time anyone had ever addressed him as "Mister."

". . . It is with profound sadness and heavy heart that I inform you of the death of your uncle, Syrus Augustus Smith, on the first day of February, this year. Please be comforted in my assurance that his many friends saw to it that he was put away with all the dignity and reverence befitting . . ."

Arnie squinted at the shaky Spencerian script. Syrus Augustus Smith. He guessed that must be his uncle Sy that he had heard his pa mention occasionally but had never met. Somehow, the knowledge that Uncle Sy had lain dead these past three months did not disturb him greatly. And he had the nagging suspicion that the writer of the letter was not unduly disturbed either, despite all the high-flown words.

The old gentleman must have been well into his seventies. To the best of Arnie's knowledge, he had lived a full and happy life. Ran a country store or some such thing. Besides all that, the letter had been resting in a pigeonhole of the Stockman's Hotel mail desk for a good part of the winter, and this seemed to dilute the aspect of tragedy.

According to your late uncle's last wish, it becomes my duty to inform you . . .

Arnie read the letter all the way through, very carefully. Then, because he was a slow and uncertain reader, he returned to the beginning and did it all over again. The printed heading on the paper stated that the writer was a lawyer by the name of Webber, and that he was a member of a firm that called itself Hinkle, Mawson, and Sylvester, in the county seat town of Placer, Texas.

The hotel clerk eyed the lanky cowhand with apprehension. It had been his experience that when a cowhand got a letter it usually contained bad news, and it was hard to guess what a hand just off the trail would do in such a case. To be on the safe side, he sidled along the desk until he was within easy reach of the shotgun that lay on the lower shelf. "It ain't bad news, I hope," he said tentatively.

Arnie looked at him blankly, and the clerk sighed to himself. The cowhand's wife had quit him and ran off with a whisky drummer he decided. His

6

sweetheart had married the banker's son. The plague had wiped out his family. The clerk moved a little closer to the shotgun. "Things ain't always as bad as they look like right at first," he said soothingly.

"Bad?" Arnie asked hollowly. All that winter the outfit had been holding a big herd in the Cherokee Outlet, hoping that beef prices in Dodge would go up. But the prices had gone down, and the settlers in the Outlet began to get ugly because they didn't like the idea of Texas cows eating all their grass. It had been a bad winter all around. Arnie's clothes were still stiff with the Outlet's red clay. Graybacks had got into his beard and hair, not to mention his clothing. And the cattle had been sold at a loss, according to the owner.

Almost six months of frustration showed in Arnie's face at that moment. The hotel clerk said quietly, "I'm sorry you got bad news, but it ain't no doin' of mine. Don't start no trouble in the hotel, I'm warnin' you."

Arnie stared at him. Slowly, he began to grin. He released the saddle that he had been carrying on his hip and let it crash to the floor. He threw back his head and whooped. "Whoo—eee! I'm rich! Belly up to the bar, boys, the drinks're on me!"

The next thing Arnie clearly remembered was waking up the following morning in the Dodge City jail. A big deputy marshal had him by the shoulders, shaking him in an offhand, bored sort of way.

"Come alive, cowboy. The judge and that saloon owner and several other people are right anxious to talk to you this morning."

Arnie stared at him blearily, fighting off the strong hands. Little by little it came back to him. After reading the letter, the first thing he had done was to go to the boss and draw his six months' pay. Then the loud hoorahing. The laughter. The drinking. *"I'm a man of property, boys! Drink 'er up!"*

"Rise an' shine," the deputy droned patiently. "The play party's over. Settlin'-up day's at hand."

Cautiously, Arnie hauled himself to a sitting position on the board bunk. His head throbbed. There was an egg-sized lump over his left cheekbone. He moved his tongue around in his mouth, checking for loose teeth.

"How long I been here?"

"Since around midnight, they say. I wasn't here at the time."

"What's the damage amount to?"

The deputy thought for a moment. "Maybe a half a dozen busted bottles of whisky. Two, three chairs, and a table—not good for anything now but kindlin' wood. Two busted windows."

"That all?"

"Well, there's a bartender with a cut over his eye. He ain't said yet if he wants to make a complaint."

Arnie felt as if his skull had been hollowed out and stuffed with gunpowder. He decided it was better not to think about the night before. Whisky, gambling, and painted women, the curse of all cowhands at the end of the trail. Better just not to think about it.

"I had six months' pay in my pocket," he said at last.

"Not any more," the deputy grinned. "The marshal took what you had and put it in his safe."

Arnie sighed. It served him right, acting the fool. Bragging how rich he was. Buying liquor for every loafer and sharpshooter that happened to walk into the saloon. He dimly recalled that somewhere along the line someone had passed a careless remark about storekeepers. Then the fandango. A roomful of drovers, their gizzards pickled in red whisky—it didn't take much to start a ruckus in that kind of company.

"Well," he told the lawman, "I guess I might as well get it over with."

The judge stared at him with sharp and humorless eyes. "What have you got to say for yourself, Smith?"

Even with a pounding head and churning innards Arnie could see that this judge would have a poor ear for excuses. He waggled a loose front tooth with his tongue and tried to gather his shattered thoughts. "Judge," he said at last, with all the sincerity he could muster, "I ain't got nothin' to say for myself at all. Except it's been a hard winter.

And yesterday was end of trail, and I guess I acted the fool."

The judge's grim expression did not change. "I take it you're prepared to settle with the saloon for the damage you caused?"

Arnie nodded and winced. "Yes, sir," he said contritely, "I'm right willin' to do that. Last night I had six months' pay in my pocket. If I could keep out enough to buy me a train ticket to a place called Smith, Texas, that would suit me fine."

The judge looked at the bartender with the discolored eye. Grudgingly, the man nodded. "The owner of the saloon will submit a bill of damages," the judge said. "When everything's settled to the plaintiff's satisfaction a deputy of the city marshal will see that you catch the first transportation out of Dodge City. Until that time you will rest in our jail. Is everything understood and agreed to?"

Arnie nodded with infinite weariness. "I reckon so."

Dodge City was not the hell-raising end-of-track town that it had once been. Years had aged and mellowed it. The citizenry had developed a fondness for peace and quiet. The rowdier element had moved on west to the Panhandle, or south to the Oklahoma country.

Arnie returned to the jail where he fell back onto the board bunk and was instantly asleep. It was near noon when he awoke again with the deputy shaking him.

"It's over and done with, cowboy. Twenty-six dollars for the damage to the saloon. Just sign your name on this paper."

Arnie stared dully at the official-looking paper. He signed it without trying to read it. "That settles you up for the saloon," the deputy told him with a grin. "Lucky for you the bartender didn't make a complaint about the cuts and bruises on his body."

Arnie did not feel particularly lucky. What he felt most of all was bruised and sick and covered with six months of cow-camp grime. "Did you get me a train ticket out of here?"

"Got you a ticket on the mud wagon to Liberal. The hack pulls out in about an hour."

It took Arnie several seconds to digest this. "I don't want to go to Liberal. I don't want to ride a mud wagon."

"Only way to do it," the deputy assured him. "At Liberal you catch the Rock Island to Caldwell. From Caldwell you get to Arkansas City somehow and catch the Santa Fe through the Oklahoma country to a place called Marietta. That's in the Chickasaw Nation."

Arnie looked at him bleakly, waiting for him to go on. "That's where your money ran out," the deputy told him pleasantly. He handed Arnie several strips of paper of assorted colors. "Here's your tickets. If I was you I'd watch out not to lose them." He flung open the cell door with a flourish.

"There you are, Smith. Free as a wild goose on the salt flats."

As Arnie was leaving the jail the deputy called, "Take a care not to miss that mud wagon."

He picked up his saddle and blanket roll and war bag at the hotel. For some time he stood forlornly on a street corner, the saddle on his shoulder, the roll under his arm. Dodge City had become so refined that the officials frowned on the wearing of firearms inside the city limits.

Beneath his shirt he could feel the grayback lice working their way over the surface of his grimy skin. They were also in his beard and hair. Arnie had never been a man to dwell at inordinate length on such subjects as personal hygiene, but at that moment he experienced an uncontrollable desire for a long hot bath and a change of clothing.

Without actually knowing how he got there, he found himself in a livery barn confronting the owner. "I want to sell my saddle. How much you figger she's worth?"

A cowhand selling his saddle—that was sinking to the final depths of degradation. It was a sure sign that he had given up all hope. He could hear his friends talking now. "I hear old Arnie Smith sold his saddle." The same as saying, "Old Arnie Smith is dead." They would stand for a moment looking mournful, and they would not mention his name again.

The liveryman studied the saddle with a gimlet

"Well," he said aloud to the cracked and scaling looking glass, "you ain't such a hard-lookin' feller after all, are you now?"

He grinned. The magic of youth washed the weariness from his face. He carefully creased his sweat-stained and sun-faded Stetson and set it jauntily on his head. "Wouldn't do," he told himself, "to land in Smith, Texas, lookin' like a common saddle tramp."

Without a saddle, he thought with fleeting bleakness. But not even that shameful fact could dampen his spirits for long. After all, he still had that letter from the Texas lawyer. His uncle had died, leaving him his country store in his will. Arnie Smith was now a property owner. And he was twenty-one years old. That was not a bad combination.

He gave the bathhouse boy a dime and said, "Bring me some bay rum, and plenty of it."

He doused the pungent lotion over his head and brushed his hair to patent leather slickness and reset his hat. "Boys," he said to the empty bathhouse, "I reckon I'm as ready as I'm goin' to get."

Back on the street, he eyed the saloons with a certain longing. After six months of cow camp, his period of celebration, expensive as it had been, seemed all too brief. But he put aside the notion of buying a drink or two of red whisky while waiting for the mud wagon. His finances had shrunk again to the danger point. He carefully counted it out— six dollars. And a few odd pieces of silver.

His stomach growled. It occurred to him that he hadn't eaten since the herd had been delivered almost twenty-four hours ago. With a sigh he passed three saloons and entered a shack that called itself the Ritz Café. "Bowl of chili," he told the counterman.

The counterman served his thick, Southwest-style chili in one bowl and a handful of oyster crackers in another. Arnie dug in. The fiery meat hit his stomach like a bullet. "Godamighty!" he gasped. After pouring a goodly amount of red vinegar into the chili to cut the grease and mitigate the fire of red peppers, he dug in again and finished the bowl. He ate the last cracker and drank the last drop of his bitter coffee. When he walked out his finances had been reduced to six dollars even.

Back at the depot the agent informed him that the mud wagon driver was still at the funeral.

Without actually thinking of what he was doing, Arnie was just pushing open the swinging doors of a saloon when the city deputy appeared at his elbow. "Sober, Smith," the big lawman said with a practiced smile. "That's how you're goin' to stay for the rest of the time you're in Dodge."

Arnie pulled himself up in outrage. "What's a man goin' to do with hisself if he can't go to a saloon?"

"Set down somewheres," the deputy told him, "and meditate, like they say. Count your blessin's."

That—since he had little or nothing to say in the

matter—was about what he did. He returned to the depot, made himself a seat on a baggage cart, and wondered idly about the country store that he had inherited. He had been in hundreds of country stores, of course, but he could honestly say that he had never given any thought to owning one. What was a store worth, anyway? he wondered. Most likely it depended on the store and where it was situated. "Ought to be worth two, three hundred dollars at least," he decided. The thought dazzled him. Two, three hundred dollars all in one bundle, stuffed into his own pocket! It was more money than he had ever imagined having at one time.

Idly, he built a cigarette and lit it. "Of course," he said aloud, wisely, "there's hard times to contend with. Better not count on more'n two hundred."

One thing he had figured on from the very beginning, from the moment he had read that lawyer's letter, and that was to sell the store and take the money and go back to doing the only thing he knew, which was working cattle. After a while he roused himself to go into the depot and ask the Santa Fe agent if he knew the whereabouts of Smith, Texas.

The agent had never heard of the place. He searched the railroad map but did not find it. Finally he consulted a directory of United States post offices, and there he found it. He returned to the map and pinpointed it, more or less, for Arnie's benefit. "There she is, over by the piney wood country, looks like, not too far from the Louisiana line."

Arnie looked closely at the dot that the agent had drawn on the map. It was placed about midway between the Sabine and the Neches. It was not cow country. Arnie had heard stories of black earth and dense forests of post oak and blackjack.

"Cotton country," the agent said in a tone of mild disdain, putting the map back on the wall.

Well, Arnie reasoned, if some folks wanted to farm for a living, he guessed that was their business. As long as they didn't expect *him* to do it. He went back to the baggage cart and smoked another cigarette and devised pleasant ways of spending the money that he would get for the store.

The mud wagon driver returned from the funeral which had thrown him an hour behind schedule. But then nobody expected a mud wagon to run on schedule.

Arnie did not find much to interest him in Liberal. It was a tame town now, like Dodge. The frontier, what was left of it, had moved on to the High Plains beyond the Cap Rock. In front of the Rock Island depot there were great rolls of barbed wire that had been shipped in from the East. It was a sad sight for a cowhand to have to look at while waiting for his train.

"I'm goin' to Smith, Texas," Arnie told the Rock Island agent. "My uncle Sy died and left me a country store. I aim to sell out soon's I can and strike west again. Cotton country ain't no place for a cowhand."

The agent was profoundly uninterested. "You got any baggage to be checked?"

Arnie's cheeks flushed with shame. A train-riding cowhand without a sacked saddle to go in the baggage car was almost unheard of. He started to make up a story about having his saddle stolen during a layover in Dodge, but the agent had already turned away and was chalking up the arrival time of the next train.

Arnie ate another bowl of chili at a café near the tracks and tried to engage the counterman in conversation. But the counterman was not interested in Smith, Texas, or country stores. It seemed a shame. After all, the place was named after his uncle. It wasn't everyone who got a place named after him.

He bought a sack of tobacco and sauntered along the quiet streets of Liberal. Being freshly out of a bathhouse and decked out in new pants and shirt, it seemed a pity not to visit one of the many friendly looking saloons. Arnie Smith bubbled with the juice of youth and was naturally drawn to places where laughter and good companionship abounded.

But he was acutely aware of the diminishing state of his finances. With a sigh of resignation he returned to the depot and slept on the hard oak bench until the eastbound train was ready to pull out.

The dusty day coach lurched and rolled on the unsettled roadbed. Arnie skillfully wedged himself into the corner of the plush seat and went back to sleep. A cowhand learned to take his sleep where he found it; on the road, in the saddle, in the rain. The conductor woke him to look at his ticket and to punch away the part that concerned him. "Layover in Caldwell till mornin'. There's a stage connection to Arkansas City where you'll take the Santa Fe to Marietta."

Arnie started to tell him that he was actually going to Smith, Texas, and not Marietta at all. It was just that his money had played out and he would have to manage the remaining distance the best way he could. But the conductor had already moved on, punching more tickets, warning more passengers about the layover.

The butcher boy came through with a basket of fruit and sandwiches and dime novels. Arnie bought a ham sandwich and ate it hungrily. The butcher returned going the other way, this time selling coffee in paper cups. Arnie bought a cup of coffee but found it too weak for his cowhand's taste. He counted his money and was appalled to discover that it had melted away to slightly less than five dollars.

The luxury of hotel sleeping was out of the question. He spent the night with two farmers in the

Caldwell depot. The next day they transferred to an ancient four-horse Abbott and Downing and struck for Arkansas City. From that point Arnie sort of lost track of time and events.

He found himself in another day coach. For a long while he stared through the grimy windows at the monotony of Cherokee grassland. The train lurched on to the south across rolling prairie, stopping for a time at the raw, new town of Oklahoma City. When Arnie became bored he braced himself in the seat, pulled his hat down over his face, and went to sleep.

Then the conductor was shaking him. "Marietta, cowboy. End of the line for you."

Marietta turned out to be a yellow Rock Island depot and a water tank, with maybe a half dozen smack-up shanties scattered carelessly on the rolling prairie. One of the shanties had the traditional square false front of a country general store, as distinctive in its way as the steeple on a church. Arnie regarded the store with unusual interest. Maybe that's what his store in Smith would look like. If he ever got to Smith.

A rickety farm wagon was pulling away from the store, clattering cross country to the south. Arnie grabbed up his blanket roll and ran after it. "Hey, mister," he hollered, "what about ridin' along with you?"

The farmer looked back at him with dull, uninterested eyes. When Arnie began to close ground between himself and the wagon, the man whipped up his team of bony mules and the wagon slowly pulled away.

"Hell and damnation!" Arnie came to a stumbling halt and puffed for breath. "That's a damn sodbuster for you! You'd think it'd take the hide right off his back to give a feller a ride!" Wearily, he hefted his blanket roll to his shoulder and headed back toward the store.

"Howdy," he grinned, regaining his good humor as he neared the store's front porch. A man on the porch stared at him blankly—he might have been the twin of the man on the wagon. "I'm headed across the Red," Arnie told him, "over towards the piney wood country in Texas. Don't reckon you know anybody goin' that way, do you?"

The man looked at him for a minute, then spat a stream of tobacco juice on the porch steps and turned away. Arnie tramped wearily up the steps and into the store. A young man about Arnie's age met him at the doorway with a weak grin. "Howdy."

Arnie brightened, pleased to find someone who would speak to him. "I just landed off the train," he told the clerk. "Hoped I'd run across somebody that would ride me a piece of the way to Red River. So far I ain't had much luck."

The young man made a sound that might have been laughter. "Folks hereabouts don't take to strangers. Hard times. Lots of drifters in the country. Best to mind their own business, they figger."

As a store owner himself, Arnie gazed about the cluttered interior with what he supposed was a professional eye. He coolly decided that, as such places went, it wasn't much. He strolled casually toward the rear of the store, between mountains of dry goods piled on tables, around buckets of onion sets and seed potatoes, over plow handles and chopping hoes and bins of brogan shoes. He gazed idly at the shuck collars swinging from the ceiling, the cheap harness, the piles of wheel spokes. Nothing here, he thought superiorly, that a self-respecting cowhand would have. Except, of course, the grub.

"Tell you the truth," he said confidentially to the clerk, "all I had to eat today was a ham sandwich and some weak coffee on the train." He pointed toward an impressive wheel of yellow cheese. "I'll take a nickel's worth of that. And a handful of crackers, and a can of sardines."

The clerk cut off a wedge of cheese and set it on the lunch counter between the meat box and pickle barrel, along with a handful of crackers and the sardines. Arnie's personal wealth was reduced by another twenty cents. He ate the cheese with relish, then opened the can and speared the tiny sardines with his barlow knife and ate them daintily one by one. When he had finished he tilted the can and drank the oil. He gazed wistfully at a stack of ginger snaps, called "smacks" by cowhands, but decided that he could not spare any more money on eating.

Up toward the front of the store an old whiskered

gaffer watched Arnie with a suspicious eye. The owner, Arnie decided. Well, if that's the way store-keeping soured a man, he sure didn't want to have anything to do with it.

In the rear of the store two farmers lounged on nail kegs beside a cold potbellied stove. They had their razor-sharp knives out, methodically reducing box pine sticks to neat piles of whisper-thin shavings. Without appearing to, they were also watching the newcomer.

Maybe times wouldn't be so hard, Arnie thought disdainfully, if you fellers would stop whittlin' long enough to get some crops planted. "How far you reckon it is to Red River?" he asked the clerk.

The clerk thought about it for a moment. "Hour, maybe. If you was horsebackin'. A good bit longer if you're afoot."

Arnie groaned to himself. "Well, if I got to walk it, I got to walk it." He picked up his roll and started to leave the store. Halfway out he was overcome by temptation. "Weigh me a nickel's worth of them smacks," he said, dragging the money out of his new California pants.

He had been walking for the best part of an hour when the wagon appeared in the north and overtook him. Arnie grinned up at the wagon's occupants, recognizing the two whittlers back at the store. "If you fellers are headed south I'd be right proud to ride along with you for a spell."

"Git in," the man with the lines told him unsmilingly.

Arnie climbed eagerly over the sideboards of the farm wagon. "I don't mind tellin' you," he told his two benefactors, "I'd just about had a bait of walkin'." He sat down on a pile of cotton bagging and rubbed his aching feet. "These boots," he said with a note of natural pride, "never was made for walkin' in. Had them special made at Ellsworth. Cost me three months' pay. But good boots don't come cheap, that's the way I look at it."

The two farmers said nothing. The wagon began jolting over an ill-defined set of tracks bearing generally south. It was then that Arnie became aware that they were looking at him in a peculiar sort of way.

For the first time Arnie gave some attention to the way the two men were dressed. Their shapeless, collarless hickory shirts. Their pants of cheap jeans material so rough that it was rarely worn without a lining. Their unfitted, hard leather brogan shoes. He began to wish that he hadn't brought their attention to the superior quality of his own boots. And he would have been easier in his mind if his pants and shirt hadn't been quite so new.

There was something in their eyes, in their unsmiling faces, as they looked at him. Arnie's thoughts began to shy off onto unpleasant side trails. His scalp prickled.

CHAPTER TWO

The first words the young man spoke were, "Sardines. Cheese. Ginger snaps." He turned to the older man. "That's livin' mighty high, I'd say."

The older man shielded his mouth with the back of his hand and spat over the side of the wagon. "New shirt," he said. "California pants. Fancy boots."

Arnie started to object. California pants were common work clothes to a cowhand, as necessary as well-fitted boots and a decent hat. But he saw by their expressions that they were in no mood to understand any of that.

The young man looked at Arnie and smiled. The expression was stiff and grim. He had not had much practice at smiling. "What's your name, cow-hand? What're you doin' here in the Chickasaw Nation with us dirt farmers?"

Arnie said with a shrug. "Name's Smith. I was headin' for Texas, but I run out of train money."

"Out of money," the young farmer echoed sourly. "But he can afford fancy grub and new duds. Don't that strike you queer, Pa?"

The older man seemed to sigh. Arnie began to think that walking wasn't such a bad idea after all. He would have gone back to it gladly if he could have thought of a graceful way of parting company with the two farmers. But he couldn't think of anything.

Talkative and friendly by nature, Arnie offered them his smoking tobacco. They shook their heads. They were chewers, not smokers. "You fellers live around here somewheres?" Arnie inquired, rolling a cigarette for himself.

"Somewheres," the young farmer said dryly.

Strangely dispirited, the young cowhand lit his cigarette and smoked in silence. He began to wonder if a country store in Texas was worth all the trouble he was going to. He longed for the rowdy companionship of cowhands. He yearned for cow camp cooking, and bitter Arbuckle's coffee, and the feel of a good working horse between his legs.

Suddenly he noticed that the wagon had left the main track and was veering uncertainly off to the east. "Say," he said, getting to his feet, "if you fellers ain't goin' on south I better get out and look for another way to travel."

"Set down," the older farmer told him coldly.

Arnie did not sit down, but neither did he try to leave the wagon. That was a mistake. The farmer stopped the mules and wrapped his lines. When he turned to face Arnie he was gripping a heavy wagon wheel spoke in one hand. The younger man's face was grim and angry. From somewhere he had picked up a broken ax handle.

The senior farmer wiped his tobacco-stained mouth and said mildly, "Rest easy, cowboy, we don't want no trouble. All we want's your money."

Arnie stared at them. "If I had any money would I of left that train when I did?"

"You had money at the store."

The young farmer hefted his ax handle threateningly. The older one said quietly, "You ain't goin' to make trouble for us, are you, cowboy?"

"Make trouble for *you!*" There was a kind of grim humor in the situation. Arnie was on the verge of laughing when the young farmer lunged at him.

The ax handle struck Arnie a glancing blow alongside the ear. His eyes were dazzled with a blinding light. He threw himself at the young farmer and was immediately hit again from the other side. The wagon wheel spoke, he thought stupidly. Shock and pain swept over him like icy water. He found himself on his hands and knees staring down at two pairs of brogan shoes. Then something hard and heavy—it must have been the ax handle—struck the back of his head.

The next thing he saw was the sandstone outcrop jutting out of the spring-green prairie. It was about a foot high, an inch or so from the tip of Arnie's nose. In his distorted vision it loomed like a mountain. He lay there for a long while, staring at the outcrop. The pain in his head went all the way to the pit of his stomach. He was cold.

It all came back to him, a little at a time and very slowly. The scuffle—all too brief—in the wagon. The hammerlike blow on the back of his head.

Here. The outcrop. The chill that lay on his body like a wet sheet.

After what must have been a long time his mind began toying with a few very small thoughts. The long, black shadow of the outcrop, for instance. He studied that for several minutes. There was no way of knowing how long he had been unconscious. But the shadow was long and it was dark. That meant the angle of the sun had dropped several degrees since the last time he had been capable of noticing such things. It was late afternoon. He had been lying unconscious in the middle of an empty prairie for almost an hour. He was absurdly proud of himself for working all that out just from the shadow of the outcrop.

He began to shiver. Lord, he thought with inde-scribable weariness, I'm *cold!*

He was cold because he had been stretched out all this time in nothing but his union suit. The farmers had stripped him of his clothing. He thought about this for several minutes. He thought about it coolly and without anger, for he quickly discovered that anger only increased the pounding in his head.

He rolled over, very carefully, and stared up at a cloudless sky. "What I got to do," he said hoarsely, "is get up from here."

It would not be easy. It would be painful and it would take hard work, but it was a task that had to be faced. There was a limit to how long a man could lie on the prairie in nothing but his union suit.

Arnie shoved himself up convulsively before he had a chance to lose his nerve. He was immediately sorry for his rashness. His stomach lurched. The horizon tilted crazily. But he was sitting upright on the tough prairie sod, and that was no small thing. He stared at his bare feet and listlessly cursed the farmers. He knew in his heart that he would never see his handcrafted footgear again.

He fumbled like a blind man, searching for his hat, for a cowhand without a hat was almost as pitiful a sight as a cowhand without his pants. The hat was gone. He looked for his new shirt and California pants. Gone. In their place, like so much trash swept out of a deserted house, was a pair of shapeless jean pants, a smocklike collarless shirt, and a pair of brogan shoes.

"Well," Arnie thought, with the hard-dying optimism of youth, "it could be worse. They could of left me nothin' at all."

But he didn't really believe that anything could be much worse than a cowhand wearing a plow hand's clothing.

Groggily, he hauled himself to his feet and, with distaste that amounted almost to nausea, pulled on the shapeless stovepipe pants. "Godamighty!" he gasped. The rough jeans material was unlined and clawed his sensitive skin like stinging nettles. "Well," he consoled himself bitterly, "it's better'n goin' naked."

But not much. Reluctantly, he pulled on the sweat-stained shirt and stepped into the iron-hard brogans.

The brogans were brutally rough and unyielding. Arnie practiced walking in them. With the care and concentration of a man crossing quicksand, he tried to discover a way of wearing them in reasonable comfort. There was no way. No matter how he laced them or how gingerly he walked in them, the wood pegs in the soles dug cruelly into his tender feet.

Exhausted, he sank to the ground and bitterly cursed his uncle for having brought him to this miserable end. If it hadn't been for the store he wouldn't have started the ruckus in Dodge. He would have gotten himself happily drunk, like any self-respecting cowhand, thrown his money away on faro and fancy women, and it would have been the end of it.

Arnie was feeling profoundly sorry for himself. Sorry for his battered and aching head. And, if the truth had been known, he was a little scared.

But the mere fact of being twenty-one years of age was in itself a medicine. After that initial fit of self-pity he hauled himself to his feet again and limped off toward the main wagon track. As he walked he fumbled futilely at the pocket of his shirt.

"Goddamn that sodbuster to everlastin' hell! He went and took my makin's!"

Arnie had been walking for less than an hour when the two-horse buggy approached him from the north. Inside the iron brogans his feet were bleeding. In his experience in cow camps and on the trail he had known periods of extreme discomfort, but he had never been as thoroughly miserable as he was now.

He stared at the distant buggy without much hope and waved forlornly.

Surprisingly, the driver of the buggy waved back. Arnie limped over to the side of the wagon track and waited with wilted spirits. "Mister," he prayed fervently, "help me get out of this country. I'll be in your debt from here on out!"

The driver hauled his two gray mules to a halt and grinned at Arnie. The young cowhand was heartened to see that he was not a sodbuster. He was a big, comfortable-looking man, well dressed. Fancy dressed, some might say. His face had the ruddy beefsteak color of a heavy drinker.

"Howdy, boy. You lookin' for a ride across the river? I wouldn't mind a little company."

Arnie heaved a great sigh of relief. "And I sure wouldn't mind settin' a while. My feet're played out, and these sodbuster pants have got me galled like a cheap saddle on a sore-back mule."

The man laughed. "Climb in. Make a place for yourself wherever you can find it." Alertly, Arnie climbed onto the buggy's leather seat and wedged himself in among a small mountain of suitcases and boxes.

"There was somethin' about you," the driver said as he whipped up the mules. "I said to myself, soon's I seen you standin' there beside the track, 'That ain't no sodbuster. In spite of the clothes he's wearin'.' " He shot Arnie a faintly curious look. "I been travelin' this post oak country longer'n I like to think about—one thing I can tell as far as I can see, is a sodbuster."

"Mister," Arnie told him with feeling, "if you had the time I could tell you the low-downest story you ever listened to."

"Time is somethin' a travelin' man's got plenty of," the driver said comfortably. "Tell away."

When Arnie reached the end of his tale of woe, the man sat back and chuckled good-naturedly. "Hard times," he said by way of explanation. "A sodbuster works all year and then watches his seeds die in the ground. Or the price of cotton goes down so he can't pay off his lien. Loses his farm and has to go to work as a tenant for somebody else. After a while he don't know which way to turn. Like a high-spirited colt that's been broke with a fence post. He turns mean."

Arnie bristled. "They never had no call to do what they did to *me*. It wasn't *me* that killed their seed or pulled the price of cotton down."

"I guess they don't stop to figger that out. When it's hard times."

33

"All I want," Arnie said bitterly, "is to get out of this country. I've seen me enough sodbusters to last a lifetime!"

"Whereabouts you headed?" the driver asked.

"Place called Smith, Texas."

The red-faced man chuckled again in his unsettling way. "Boy," he said sincerely, "where you're goin', you've got a heap to learn about sodbusters." He pointed ahead toward a thin stand of timber. "That's Red River. We'll make camp on the north bank tonight and cross in the mornin'."

Arnie sat for a while in vaguely troubled silence. The driver looked at him "Somethin' bitin' you, boy."

"Well . . ." Arnie shrugged. "After what's happened to me, I guess it's give me a suspicious mind. It kind of makes me wonder why you're bein' so accommodatin'."

The big driver smiled quietly and did not seem offended. "Boy," he said, "when I told you a while back that I wouldn't mind some company, I was tellin' you the Lord's truth. Lonesome business, travelin'. Long stretch between settlements here in the post oak country."

"I guess," Arnie said. "But how'd you know I wouldn't knock you on the head, first chance I got, and rob you?"

"Guess I didn't know. Not for sure."

"It didn't worry you?"

"Not much," the big stranger shrugged.

"Hardware's my line. And a travelin' man has to know his line if he wants to stay in business." He pulled back his coat and showed Arnie a dark, businesslike revolver strapped over his vest in a shoulder holster.

"A gun drummer." Arnie stared at him with new respect and a little awe. He had seen gun drummers shoot spinning silver dollars right out of the air. He had seen them shoot through knotholes in planks without touching the wood. It was their business. "Well," Arnie grinned weakly, "I guess a gun drummer's a good man to pard with in this country."

"It depends," the man said quietly, draping his coat over the slight bulge. "It all depends."

They made camp that night on the wide sandy bank of the Red. "Name's Hefford," the stranger said as Arnie helped him unhitch the mules. "Bob Hefford."

"Arnie Smith," Arnie told him. "I'm right proud to meet you."

Hefford took the mules to water while Arnie gathered driftwood and started the fire. They cooked thick slabs of salt pork, then made skillet bread out of corn meal and a little water and cooked it in the meat grease. Hefford rustled two cans of tomatoes out of his buggy supplies and they wolfed them with the meat and bread. Capped with a pot of bitter Arbuckle's, it was a feast.

Grinning, Arnie belched and patted his stomach. "Best grub I've et since we quit the trail at Dodge."

"I've been wonderin'," Hefford said. "What's a cowhand doin' in post oak and cotton country?"

Pleased to find someone who would listen to him, Arnie retold the entire story of his inheritance, the ruckus in Dodge, and the journey that had followed, winding up with the two sodbusters and disaster. They let the fire die down and sat back and listened for a while to the sounds of the night.

"How," Arnie said idly, "does a body get to be a gun drummer?"

Hefford leaned back on one of his pasteboard display cases and gazed at the darkness. He said nothing. After a while Arnie realized that he wasn't going to say anything. "I didn't aim to ask questions out of turn," Arnie said at last.

"That's all right. It was a natural question." Hefford went on gazing at the darkness beyond the fire. He didn't seem angry. But he didn't answer Arnie's question. "I've got a spare blanket in the buggy," he said. "Better throw our beds before long. Get an early start across the river in the mornin'."

After throwing their blankets next to the fire Hefford opened one of his cases and took out a bottle of whisky. He held it to the red light of the fire and looked at it thoughtfully. "A little somethin'," he said, "to hold off the chill."

Gratefully, Arnie accepted the proffered bottle.

After all he had been through that day he felt that he deserved a little dram of something to warm his innards. Something to take his mind off his tender feet.

He gasped as the fiery liquid hit his stomach. His eyes watered. He experienced a sudden difficulty in breathing. What had just gone down his throat was the rawest and cheapest kind of white corn whisky. Somehow Arnie had expected better from a man like Bob Hefford. He returned the bottle with a shaking hand.

Hefford smiled faintly. "I guess I ain't very particular about the kind of liquor I drink." He turned the bottle up and gulped several times without batting an eye. He didn't even seem to taste it. Arnie shook his head when he was offered the bottle a second time.

"It's been a long day for me. I think I'll turn in."

Arnie sat on the ground and took off the hated brogans and jean pants before sliding between the blankets. The last he saw of Hefford that night, the gun drummer was turning the bottle up for the third time.

The next morning they cooked breakfast, hitched up the team, and started across the river. "Not much rain this spring," Hefford said as the buggy entered the shallow water. "Good for crossin' rivers but hard on sodbusters." He directed the mules expertly from sandbar to sandbar, never hitting water more than hub deep. "So you're Syrus Smith's nephew," he said idly, as the mules dragged the heavy buggy up on the Texas bank. "I didn't know the old coot was dead."

Arnie squinted at him. "Died towards the first of the year. Did you know my uncle?"

"Sold your uncle an order of cheap pistols once. And a batch of two-dollar shotguns with faulty breeches. Haven't been back since then. Most likely there's some sodbusters goin' around with no eye on the right side of their face, because of them breeches." He glanced at Arnie. "You don't look much like him. Your uncle."

Arnie shrugged. "I don't know. I never seen him. He was my pa's brother, and they never got on very good."

"You know anything about runnin' a store?"

"No, sir, I sure don't. I'm sellin' out just as quick as I can find somebody to take it off my hands. Goin' back to cattle."

The buggy moved slowly out of the river bottom. Somehow Arnie always expected the Texas side of the river to look different from Indian Territory, but it never did. "Runnin' a store," Hefford said, gazing out at the green prairie, "ain't the simple thing some folks figger it is. Takes a toughness that most folks shy away from. Takes a good eye. The knack of sizing a man up on the spot, figgerin' what he's worth. Takes a feel for the ground, and growin' things, and the weather. Since I been travelin' I've seen store owners of all kinds you can think of, but I never seen a simple one. Not if he stayed in business any length of time."

"What kind of a man was my uncle?" Arnie asked, more to keep up the conversation than because he had any real interest in the late Syrus Augustus Smith.

"Syrus?" Hefford smiled faintly. "Hardmouthed as a Arkansas mule, for one thing. And tough as them brogan shoes you're wearin'. Like as not most of the sodbusters hated his guts when he died. With reason, maybe. Just the same, the store's what kept them goin'. It gave them credit when they'd of starved without it. It bought their cotton when nobody else would have it. It bought their eggs and butter and pecans at Christmas time. But the sodbusters won't recollect much of that, I guess. What'll stick in their minds is the high interest he charged them, and the liens he took on their places, and the foreclosures." Suddenly he turned to Arnie and looked faintly startled at his own flow of words. "I didn't aim to go on about it. It's like I said yesterday—travelin's a lonely business."

"I don't mind," Arnie said generously, although in truth he would have to admit that the subject of storekeeping was an extraordinarily boring one. "What kind of guns do you sell?" he asked, hoping to shift the conversation to more interesting things.

Bob Hefford's face became curiously slack. "Cheap pistols, mostly. And single-barrel shotguns that'll likely blow up in your face if you ain't careful. Not much call for rifles in the post oaks."

Arnie thought of his own pistol and saddle that he had been forced to sell. But that was too painful a subject to bring up in conversation.

Hefford guided the buggy onto a new set of wagon tracks that meandered southward across the prairie. As more fences were built, the roads kept changing. Arnie realized that Smith was far to the east somewhere and he ought to think about finding a way to get there. But for the moment it was comfortable in the buggy and he sensed a kind of security in Bob Hefford's massive presence, and in his quiet voice, and the smile that came at times so unexpectedly.

Toward midday they raised a familiar square-fronted building in the distance. "That's Giffard's Store," Hefford said. "I come this way three, four times a year. Don't look like much now, does it?"

Arnie shook his head. It was one of the most deserted places he could remember seeing. A ramshackle wagon and two dispirited mules stood forlornly in the store yard—there was no other sign of life. Two wavery sets of wagon ruts met in front of the store and then wandered uncertainly across the prairie. In official maps of the area those wagon tracks were listed as major stage roads, but Arnie didn't know that.

"Old Dan Giffard's got one of the best stores in

the post oaks," Hefford said comfortably. "Always good for an order of pistols and shells. Young bloods hereabouts figger it's the same as goin' naked as to go without a pistol in their pocket."

Arnie stared at the store but could not believe that it was anything special. It might have been the twin to the store in Marietta. "On Saturdays," Hefford went on, "there's maybe forty, fifty wagons crowded all together there in the store yard. Every wagon packin' away grub and goods worth maybe five, six dollars on the books. Add interest and credit charges to that. Figger it up yourself."

Arnie tried halfheartedly to add it up in his head. "I guess it's a lot of money, all right," he admitted. "If the storekeeper ever gets it."

Hefford smiled his strange smile. "He'll get it. One way or another." He pulled the buggy up in the wide area of dust and gravel in front of the store. "I go on south from here. You want me to ask Giffard if he knows of anybody headed towards Smith?"

"I'd be much obliged. I'll water the mules while you talk business in the store."

After he had attended to the team, Arnie wandered aimlessly about the dusty store yard. During the past twenty hours or so that he had been with Hefford he had come to think of the big drummer as a friend. He wished there was some way that they could ride on together, talking comfortably when they felt like it, making camp when the notion overtook them. But of course that was impossible. He was a man with responsibilities now. He was a store owner.

If I ever get to the damn store, he thought wearily.

A farmer came out of Giffard's, rattled quickly down the porch steps, and made for the wagon. He whipped up his mules and in a matter of minutes he had fogged it out of the store yard. Arnie cocked his head curiously.

He went over to the store porch, climbed the steps, and put his head in the doorway. Hefford had two gun cases open on a dry goods table, quietly talking to a stooped, egg-headed little man that Arnie took for the owner, Dan Giffard. The little storekeeper was nodding his head up and down, his eyes bulging slightly. He was quick to agree with everything Hefford said, although he didn't seem to be listening to his words. Two young men—store clerks, Arnie guessed—hovered in the shadows in back of the store. They seemed to be very busy without actually doing anything.

Arnie came on into the store and stood beside a dry goods table to listen to the gun drummer's spiel. "Well . . ." Hefford was saying, with just the faintest note of disapproval, "of course you know your own customers, Mr. Giffard. You know what they want and can afford. If you say the Harrington-Richardson, why of course that's fine with me, and we'll write up the order . . ."

Interested, Arnie moved a little closer. Although no self-respecting cowhand would admit to owning a Harrington-Richardson pistol, it was a well-known weapon. It was flashy with nickel plating, which the young sodbusters liked. Widely known as the "nigger killer," it was double-acting, .32 caliber, and wholesaled for $2.98. It was famous for firing its short bullet sidewise and, occasionally, blowing up in the user's hand. It was a favorite of storekeepers because the margin of profit on the weapon was well over one hundred per cent, not counting interest and credit charges.

"For myself," Hefford continued in his quiet tone, "I prefer the Iver-Johnson. It is double-acting, inexpensive, reliable." He demonstrated how snugly the Iver-Johnson slipped into the hip pocket. "Of course," he said doubtfully, "there's the American Bulldog, wholesaling at a dollar and a quarter when purchased in lots of one dozen . . ."

In distress, Mr. Giffard shook his head. The Bulldog was not popular with store owners. Neither was the Iver-Johnson. The margin of profit was too low.

Hefford rummaged through one of his black cases and drew out two Iver-Johnsons, one with a walnut handle, one with rubber. "Take my word for it, Mr. Giffard, you can't get a better little pistol for the money." He took a box of cartridges from his vest pocket and loaded both weapons. "Would you please let me have a small box of that Garrett's snuff, Mr. Giffard?"

The storekeeper got the snuff and handed it to Hefford. The gun drummer put a dime on the counter. "I used to use a silver dollar for this," he smiled. "But that was before hard times. Arnie, would you take this and come outdoors with me for a minute?"

Startled, Arnie accepted the snuff box, which was slightly larger than a half dollar. He followed Hefford out to the front porch, aware of the buzz of excitement from the two clerks. The gun drummer glanced at Arnie and said, "Toss it up in the air, boy. Throw it as high as you can."

Arnie obliged by winding up stickball fashion and throwing the snuff box almost straight up. Casually, Hefford raised the pistol in his right hand and fired. They saw the small snuff box jump as the bullet struck it. A brownish whisper of powdered tobacco drifted away on the spring breeze. Hefford fired again, and again the snuff box jumped crazily in midair. When the box hit the ground, he fired a third time, and it jumped back into the air. Then he lifted the pistol in his left hand and began firing with it. When he had finished there was not enough of the snuff box left to identify.

Hefford looked at the little storekeeper and smiled gently. "Between you and me, I wouldn't want to try that with a Harrington-Richardson."

As if in some miraculous way a small crowd had

materialized at the end of the porch after Hefford's first shot. A black field hand, a shoe drummer, a part-time blacksmith, and two tenant farmers—they had all been out of sight in one of the small sheds behind the store when the shooting had first started. They stared at Hefford with bugging eyes.

"Of course," Hefford said innocently to Mr. Giffard, "if you want to get me another box of Garrett's, I'll *try* it with the Harrington-Richardson."

The little storekeeper shook his head wearily. "No need to bother. Bring your order book inside the store and I'll make out a list."

The field hand loped down the road and recovered the battered snuff box and brought it back. Everybody gathered around and stared at it in awe. "If he can do a thing like that to a little old snuff box, think what he could do to a man!"

The young store clerk tugged at Arnie's sleeve and led him to the far end of the porch. "One thing you got to say for Mr. Hefford, he sure livelies up the day when he comes." The youth's eyes shone with excitement. "Are you a pal of his?"

"Not a pal exactly. He picked me up in the Chickasaw Nation and rode me across the river." Arnie glanced at the men who were still gaping at the snuff box. "I never seen a man that could shoot the way he does. Does he come this way often?"

The clerk shot Arnie a suspicious look. "You don't know who he is?"

"Bob Hefford. That's what he told me."

"Robert Wakefield Hefford," the clerk said softly, as if each word were a bomb. "You don't know *who* he is?"

The name rang faintly in Arnie's memory. Robert Wakefield Hefford. He didn't know any cattlemen by that name, or famous baseball players, or bare-knuckle fighters, or anybody like that. Still, the name was faintly familiar. Suddenly he brightened. "I recollect now. Ain't he the lawman . . . ?"

The young clerk nodded eagerly. "*Used* to be a lawman. Ain't any more. Won't nobody have him—folks are more scared of Robert Wakefield Hefford than of the outlaws they used to hire him to catch. That's how come he's peddlin' these cheap pistols for a livin'."

Now it was coming to Arnie. Hickok, Earp, and Hefford—those famous law names had been grouped together once. Of course Hefford had come later, well after the day of Earp and Hickok, after the frontier was already beginning to change.

Arnie turned and stared at the store where Hefford and the little storekeeper were still talking. "I'll be damned," he said, properly impressed. "All this time I been ridin' with a famous killer and never knowed anything about it."

He edged along the porch and peered through the doorway into the dark interior of the store. Hefford had his order book out, propped on a bolt of striped hickory, carefully recording the model numbers as Mr. Giffard called them out.

"Tell you the truth," the clerk said quietly, with a secret grin, "I don't mind much *who* he is, or *what* he's done. He never shot anybody that *I* know." He moved closer and lowered his voice to a whisper. "You know how many of them Iver-Johnson pistols old Giffard's got back in the shed room still in the boxes, that ain't never been opened?"

Arnie looked at him blankly. "Four dozen!" The clerk grinned from the side of his mouth. "Every time Hefford comes through he writes up another order. The store buys twice as many pistols as it sells. Pretty soon we'll have as many Iver-Johnsons as the factory."

Arnie was puzzled. "Why does he buy the pistols if he can't sell them?"

"Figgers it's good for his health not to ruffle the gun shark's feathers. Reckon I'd do the same, if I was in his place."

"Do all the storekeepers buy from him just because of his reputation?"

The young man shrugged and spread his hands in classical shopkeeper fashion. "Wouldn't you?"

Would he? Arnie didn't know. One day—providing he ever actually got to Smith—he might have the opportunity to find out.

CHAPTER THREE

Hefford came down the steps with his sample case and order books. The small crowd that had gathered for the sharpshooting exhibition had melted away; Arnie stood alone in the store yard alongside the drummer's mules.

"Hard luck," Hefford said, as he heaved his sample cases into the buggy. "Old Giffard don't know anybody headin' east today. But you can lay over till tomorrow—sleep in the blacksmith shed in back of the store. Sooner or later somebody'll come along."

Arnie shrugged dejectedly. "I guess."

"If I had the time," Hefford told him, "I could ride you over to Cross Oaks, on the main stage road to Louisiana. Plenty of freighters and such like headed east." He smiled faintly. "But Cross Oaks is almost a day out of my way."

"I'll be all right," Arnie assured him.

"Well . . ." The gun drummer held out a lean, surprisingly smooth hand and they shook. "I better get started."

"Much obliged for the ride. And for the supper last night."

Hefford climbed into the heavy buggy and hollered at the mules. Arnie stood alone and forlorn in the middle of the store yard watching the buggy draw slowly away. He tried to reassure himself with a cocky grin, but in his heart he felt that he was losing a friend. It didn't matter if his name was Robert Wakefield Hefford, a rogue lawman; a gun drummer whose stock in trade was fear and intimidation. The fact remained that Hefford's was the only truly friendly face that Arnie had seen since leaving Dodge.

To Arnie's surprise the buggy slowed down and stopped in the middle of that deep-rutted road. Hefford twisted around in the seat and looked back at him. "Well," he called with a hint of a sigh, "you might as well get in."

"You changed your mind about headin' south?"

"I ain't changed my mind. But a travelin' man's got plenty of time. If the mules don't mind takin' a side track to Cross Oaks, I reckon I don't."

For cross country travel the heavy buggy was relatively comfortable. Arnie sat back and enjoyed the scenery as it crept slowly by—the patchy black and red earth, the green prairie, the dense thickets of post oak. In the distance he glimpsed an occasional small bunch of cattle. But this was not really cattle country; mostly it was fenced farm land, and would become more so as he moved on to the east. He felt like a soldier who had, for some unexplainable reason, suddenly discovered himself far behind the lines in enemy country.

Twice that afternoon they met rickety farm wagons on the road, and long-faced sodbusters glared at them with dull, angry eyes. "Ain't there

49

anybody in this part of the country that will give you a pleasant look or a kind word?" Arnie asked.

"Hard times," Hefford said, in what seemed to be the stock explanation for all unpleasantness. "I guess they don't feel much like bein' pleasant or kind."

Shortly before sundown Hefford pointed to a distant tin roof of a cotton gin. "There she is, Cross Oaks. What there is of it." The closer they came to the small town the quieter Hefford became. He seemed to draw into himself; even his eyes seemed to be looking inward.

"Maybe," Arnie said hopefully, "you can sell some guns here. To kind of pay for goin' so far out of your way."

Hefford smiled in a strange way. "No, I don't expect I'll sell any guns in Cross Oaks."

As they drew nearer Arnie could see there wasn't really much to the town. The cotton gin, a general store, and a few small shops. There wasn't even a saloon or an eating house that Arnie could see—not that he had any money for eating or drinking.

Hefford felt in his vest pocket and drew out two silver dollars. "Here," he said to the surprised Arnie, and dropped the two coins in his hand. "It ain't more'n a day or so on to Smith, but you'll need money for grub. You can pay me later."

Considering all that he had already accepted from the drummer, Arnie was ashamed to take this latest gift of cash. On the other hand his stomach had been growling emptily for some time. "I'll send it to you as soon as I get to Smith."

The drummer shrugged. "Send it to the company in Nashville. They'll know where to find me." He turned the buggy toward the hitch rack in front of the store. "The best place to sleep is in the seed house over at the gin." Without another word he got out of the buggy and went into the store.

Arnie wandered aimlessly about the town. It didn't take long to see everything worth looking at. As soon as the sun went down the few people who lived in Cross Oaks went to their homes. Only the general store still showed a light in its windows, and Arnie headed instinctively in that direction.

The drummer's buggy was still at the rack, otherwise the street was deserted. For some time Arnie had been thinking about the abrupt way that Hefford had parted company and wondering if somehow he had offended him without knowing it. Well, he thought with the directness of youth, the best way to find out is to ask.

He walked into the crowded clutter of the store and knew immediately that something was wrong. A silence, heavy and oppressive, was in the air. A grim-faced storekeeper stood behind the counter with both hands on the wheel of a coffee grinder. He glanced at Arnie but did not speak. In the back of the store a clerk was busily arranging and re-arranging a display of needles and colored threads in a glass-topped case.

Arnie cleared his throat. "I was lookin' for Mr. Hefford."

Hefford called from some distant part of the store. "Back here, boy. In the shed room."

Arnie sidled cautiously around the cluttered goods tables and showcases. He started to smile at the storekeeper and was suddenly shocked at the naked hatred that looked back at him. The man did not speak, but his burning eyes followed Arnie the length of the store, and it was with relief that Arnie ducked in the shed room.

There Hefford was sitting on a molasses keg, a meal of canned salmon, crackers, and cheese laid out in front of him on a goods box. There was a bottle of whisky in his hand. "You lookin' for me, boy?" he asked slowly and distinctly—a little too slowly and distinctly for a man completely sober.

"I guess I was," Arnie confessed. "I don't want to be any more bother to you, but I couldn't help wonderin' if I'd said or done somethin' to get you mad."

"Mad?" Hefford blinked quickly and took a drink from the bottle. "If that's what's botherin' you, put your mind at rest." He waved toward the untouched food on the goods box. "Now that you're here, you might as well set down and have some supper."

Arnie didn't need a second invitation; he quickly pulled up another keg and dug into the salmon with his pocketknife. Hefford watched him with a crooked grin. He took another drink of whisky but did not offer any to Arnie. "Boy," he said with alcoholic preciseness, "I'm startin' to wonder if it was hard luck for me that we ever met up."

Arnie blinked, his mouth full of salmon and crackers. "I hope not. It was good luck for me."

"Meetin' up with Bob Hefford's never good luck for anybody," the drummer said. "I guess you seen that storekeeper as you came in."

"The one that looks like a mule just tromped on his corn?"

Hefford smiled slackly. "Don't blame him for the way he looks; he's got his reason for hatin' me." He started to tilt the bottle, then at the last minute changed his mind. "Three years ago I killed a man in this store—he was that storekeeper's brother-in-law."

Arnie sat for a moment, his mouth full of salmon and cheese. "If I'd knowed that," he said at last, "I never would of let you go to all the trouble of bringin' me here."

"It don't matter. Cross Oaks or somewheres else, they're all the same. Sooner or later I run into somebody—a brother, a cousin, a friend of some hard-case that I caught and sent to prison, or maybe had to kill. Lucky for me, most of them are like that storekeeper. They cuss me with their looks and stir up trouble if they can, but none of them has got the stomach to draw on a man like Bob Hefford." He held the whisky up to the reddish lamplight. "Maybe someday they will. But not yet."

Arnie gulped some more salmon and wiped his mouth with the back of his hand. "Why do you stay on in this part of the country, knowin' the way folks feel about you?"

"Habit, I guess. I was born and raised over by the piney woods. Anyhow, this is where the company sent me when they put me to sellin' their pistols. Another job wouldn't be easy to come by nowadays." He ate a small piece of cheese and washed it down with whisky. "I think I've had about enough of this place," he said suddenly. "You ready to get yourself bedded down?"

"Any time it suits you."

Hefford corked the whisky bottle. He walked out of the store, swaying slightly, scattering some silver on the counter as he passed by. The storekeeper did not say a word. If looks could have killed, Hefford never would have made it out of the shed room—but that was as far as it went.

Outside, they stood for a moment on the store porch. "Tomorrow or the next day you'll be in Smith," Hefford said. "A store of your own."

"But not for long," Arnie promised. "Just till I can get it off my hands."

Hefford grunted, perhaps thinking of his own youth. Then he held out his hand. "*Hasta luego.* Maybe we'll meet up again sometime."

Arnie was surprised. "I thought you was layin' over tonight in Cross Oaks."

"I don't feel right comfortable in towns." They shook hands quickly. "Mind what I told you about the seed house—it's the best place hereabouts for sleepin'."

With no further word Hefford climbed into his heavy duty buggy and drove away. The storekeeper crept to the doorway and watched him, his face stiff with hate.

Cross Oaks in the morning was a place of surprising activity. Arnie, burrowed comfortably into a mountain of cotton seed, could hear the sound of wagoners preparing to pull out. He sat up, stretching, yawning, using his fingers to comb tufts of lint out of his hair. From somewhere the aroma of strong bitter coffee drifted into the musty smelling seed house.

Arnie sniffed hungrily. He pulled on the hated brogans and rough jean pants and blundered out of the dark seed house to have a look at Cross Oaks by daylight.

A group of wagoners was cooking breakfast in the gin yard where they had camped. Arnie approached them with a grin. "Howdy. I smelled your coffee over in the seed house. That's where I slept last night." He stood waiting for somebody to invite him to get a plate and help himself. Among cattlemen, feeding strangers was the most natural thing in the world—it went without saying that any passer-by was welcome to whatever grub there was at hand. A cowman, of course, never dug in without an invitation.

The wagoners looked at him dully. "Looks like a good day for bein' on the road," Arnie observed brightly. "I'm headed for Smith, myself. Any you fellers know where it is?"

The wagoners—there were four of them— seemed to be listening to some distant sound that only they could hear. They chewed listlessly on their breakfast of pan bread and molasses and fried meat. Arnie's mouth began to water. Still no one invited him to eat. "Like I say," Arnie tried again, "a place called Smith is where I'm headed. It's over to the east somewheres, I don't know just where. Any of you fellers headed in that direction?"

One of the wagoners raised his head and looked at him. "Why?"

Arnie was stunned at the bad manners of these men. If this had been a camp of cowhands they would all have been as friendly as blood cousins by this time. In desperation he tried another tack. "I wouldn't be against payin' for the chance of ridin' along with you—if there's anybody here headed east."

For the first time they began to look interested. "How much?" one of them asked.

"Well," Arnie admitted, embarrassed, "all I got is two dollars."

One of the men sopped the last of his molasses out of his tin and stuffed the morsel in his mouth.

"Smith is a long piece off. Two dollars ain't much."

Arnie's face flushed angrily. His long association with cowmen had not prepared him for this kind of meanness. "Never mind," he told them shortly and started to limp off in his heavy brogans.

"If two dollars is all you got, I guess it will have to do," the wagoner said grudgingly.

"All the way to Smith?" Arnie asked suspiciously.

"Most ways. I got an order to let off at Placer. You can catch a ride from there without any trouble."

Arnie thought about it for a moment. Placer was where the lawyer was—the one called Webber. It might be a good thing to get the legal end of the inheritance straightened out before going on to Smith. "Throw in some grub," he told the wagoner, "for what time we're on the road, and it's a deal."

It was taking a little time, but he was learning. If meanness was the only thing they understood, then he would be mean.

The wagoner's name was Kramer. He was a stolid, brooding man whose job it was to transport goods from the Katy railhead to various towns and country stores in the post oaks. When he had satisfied himself that two dollars was all his passenger had he became a little less hostile. "Rich land," he said once as the heavy Studebaker jolted over the rolling black-earth prairie. "Good for cotton, corn. Most everything." He pointed a bony finger. "Had a place over there past the rise once. But the dry-up come and the crops blowed away. Had to look for somethin' else to do." He offered Arnie a chew from a twist of black tobacco. Arnie declined with thanks. The wagoner fixed his small gray eyes on Arnie while he worried a piece of tobacco from the twist. "Somehow," he said at last, "you don't look like a sodbuster."

"I ain't," Arnie told him with what he considered justifiable pride. To help pass the time he told Kramer some of his recent adventures.

The wagoner was not impressed. "It's to be expected," he said, with a surprising turn for philosophy. "When hard times come, folks turn mean." He turned his head and spat with the wind. "Say you're headed for Smith?"

"That's right. You acquainted with the place?"

"Poor country," Kramer said dispiritedly. "Three years ago the cotton burned out. Corn died in the ground. They ain't made a decent crop since."

This piece of news did not do much to boost Arnie's sagging spirits. He gazed out at the bleak landscape as the wagon jolted over the all but impassable road. All he could see was post oaks and dusty black earth as dry as gunpowder.

Late that afternoon the earth began to turn red in spots, but otherwise it all looked the same to Arnie. Occasionally they would see a shack in the distance leaning sadly with the wind, and a small piece of farm land that had been hacked out of the dense thickets of scrub timber. A fair number of the shacks appeared to be deserted. Weeds and post oak seedlings were beginning to take the farms.

Arnie gazed at the desolate scene but made no comment. He knew what the wagoner would say. Hard times.

They raised Placer about an hour before sundown, and it was a disappointment to Arnie. Somehow he had expected more from a county seat town than two cotton gins and a dozen unpainted stores. Kramer drove around to the back of the general store to unload his order. The wagoner looked around at the place and cursed. "Used to be a right smart little town here. But that was some time ago. Before hard times took it."

Arnie said his good-bys and walked off before he could hear any more.

What appeared to be the main offices of Hinkle, Mawson, and Sylvester were located on the second floor of a building that also housed a meat market and a feed store. Arnie climbed the outside stairway, eying the scaling sign on the window. He cleaned a small place on the window and peered inside. A man was working at a roll-top desk in one corner of the small room. The rest of the room looked as if a windstorm had just passed through scattering books and papers and furnishings about in imaginative patterns. Arnie opened the door and asked, "Is this the place that Hinkle, Mawson, and Sylvester are headquartered?"

A bright, birdlike little man looked at Arnie and beamed. "Bless you, Hinkle and Mawson have been dead these twenty years, young man, and two years ago Mr. Sylvester went back to his folks in Ohio." With one hand he made a flapping little sign of welcome. "Come in. Sit down. What can I do for you?"

"I ain't sure," Arnie said cautiously, sidling into the room. "I'm lookin' for a gent called . . ." He took out the letter and studied it blankly. "Called Webber."

"That's me, young sir, Herbert Webber. All that's left of Hinkle, Mawson, and Sylvester." He sighed, then smiled brightly. He swept some papers from an oak armchair and they fluttered to the floor. "Please sit down, Mr. . . ."

"Smith," Arnie said, sinking wearily onto the chair. "Arnie Smith."

Mr. Herbert Webber nodded brightly. "Ah, yes, the late Syrus Smith's nephew. I've been expecting you." He chuckled to himself as he took Arnie's hand and wrung it enthusiastically. "A sad thing," he said happily. "Your uncle was an important man, Mr. Smith. Many friends. Great loss. He was up in years, of course." He paused for a moment, smiling. "I suppose you've already been to the store and checked everything over with Purdy."

"No sir, I just landed in Placer from a place called Cross Oaks. Who's Purdy?"

Mr. Webber looked stunned, as if he couldn't

believe there was a person alive who didn't know who Purdy was. "Harve Purdy, of course, your uncle's chief clerk. Knows as much about that store and the books as anybody alive. More, now that Mr. Syrus is gone. He's been runnin' things since your uncle . . ." He smiled and shrugged his bony shoulders. Mr. Webber didn't like talking about death, although it was largely his stock in trade. "Somebody had to keep it going."

"Why?" Arnie asked. He wasn't sure that he liked the idea of a perfect stranger running his store all this time without his even knowing about it.

Arnie's blunt question seemed to shock the little lawyer. "I can understand that all this must seem strange to you, Mr. Smith. But a store like your uncle's, it can't just be closed down. Folks couldn't do without it."

"One country store is pretty much like another, as far as I can see. What makes my uncle's place so important that it couldn't be shut down?"

Mr. Webber bugged his eyes. His mouth came open and he groped for words with which to explain the situation to this young stranger who now was his client. But at the moment the under-taking was obviously too much for him "Mr. Smith," he said at last, "I can see that you don't understand. Explaining the store is going to take some time. Are you laying over at the hotel tonight?"

"No, sir," Arnie told him, "I ain't." Then, in a

weary voice, he began the story of his troubled journey from Dodge to Placer.

The lawyer listened with a slightly dazed expression. For the first time he seemed to notice the shabbiness of his client's dress. "I see," Mr. Webber said, his head bobbing up and down as Arnie dragged his tragic tale to a limping halt. "Well, you'll have supper with me and my wife, then we'll talk about the store and see about getting you a room. There's a northbound stage tomorrow morning—I expect you'll want to get on to Smith."

Arnie smiled wanly. "I ain't got any money for a stagecoach."

"The driver will be glad to trust you till you get to the store. Besides being a store owner now, you're also a postmaster and stage agent, among other things I thought you knew."

"No, sir," Arnie said with deep feeling. "I sure didn't." He thought of all the miles he had walked and the beating he had taken, when all the time he could have been riding.

Mrs. Herbert Webber was a plump, cheerful woman with apple cheeks, an easy laugh, and a talent for making men comfortable. Arnie stuffed himself on fried steak and biscuits and dried apple cobbler. "Ma'am," Arnie told her, patting his stomach, "that's the best grub I've et since way back in the Indian Territory when the outfit had a Mex cook by the name of Paco."

Mrs. Webber graciously accepted this as a compliment and laughed. Then Arnie and the lawyer moved from the kitchen to the parlor of the small Webber home, and Webber lit the lamps and began sorting through a dismaying array of legal papers. "I've got a few things for you to sign. We might as well get them out the way first thing."

Arnie accepted some of the papers and looked at them. All the long words made his head ache. The fine print made his eyes water. "Maybe you better just tell me what they're about."

With a look of mild disapproval, the lawyer adjusted his spectacles, brought one of the papers into focus, and began to read in a stupefying monotone. After the first sentence Arnie's mind began to wander. He thought about Robert Wakefield Hefford and wondered idly what the gun drummer might be doing at this moment. He thought of the two sodbusters who had attacked and robbed him—it all seemed so long ago that he could no longer work up much anger about it. He even found himself accepting what was evidently the universal explanation for every violent act. Hard times.

The lawyer lowered the paper and looked at Arnie. "If the terms are understood and agreed to, sign here." He indicated the line at the bottom of the document where Arnie was to sign.

Arnie's mind was an embarrassed blank. He had no idea what all the legal verbiage meant, but he was ashamed to admit that he had not been paying attention. He frowned wisely for several seconds, then cocked his head and asked, "What do you think?"

"The form is standard. I believe everything is in order."

"All right, I'll sign." He took an old-fashioned quill pen from the lawyer and, after a few false starts, scrawled his name on the line. Webber took up another paper and began to read. Arnie's thoughts flew immediately to a red-haired saloon girl that he had once known in Caldwell. Brickyard McCarstairs she had called herself. Arnie smiled. Absently, he took the paper from Webber when the reading had ended and signed his name. Brickyard McCarstairs had had a red and green garter tattooed around her left leg, above the knee, and above that the word "Bob." Arnie had never got around to asking who "Bob" might be, and Brickyard had never said.

After a while Mrs. Webber brought in a pot of strong coffee; not as strong as cow camp coffee, but strong enough for Arnie to appreciate. So Arnie sat in a comfortable daze, drinking coffee and listening idly to the drone of the lawyer's voice, and now and then signing another paper. At last Mr. Webber arranged all the papers in a neat stack, removed his spectacles, and smiled widely.

"That's all there is to it, Mr. Smith. You are now the legal owner of the Smith General Mercantile

Company and may take charge any time you wish."

"That's fine," Arnie said. But, in fact, he was a little disappointed. Like crossing Red River and expecting the Texas side to look different from the Indian Territory side, he had somehow expected the property-owning Arnie Smith to be different from the cowhand Arnie Smith. But he felt just the same.

"How long," he asked the lawyer, "do you figger it'll take to get it off my hands?"

Mr. Webber looked blank. "Get it off your hands?"

"Sell it. I don't know nothin' about runnin' a store. The quicker I can find a buyer, the better all around. I was hopin' you'd help me out in locatin' somebody that wanted a store."

The little lawyer's eyes bulged. He opened his mouth but made no sound. Arnie, noticing nothing wrong, continued in his rambling way. "I ain't lookin' to get rich or anything like that. All I want is enough to get me a middlin' horse and a saddle, and a stage ticket back west as far as the Panhandle. If there's anything left over, that's fine and dandy. But I'll tell you the truth, Mr. Webber; this here ain't my kind of country. The sooner I get back to where I belong the better I'll like it. So I don't aim to do any hard horse tradin'. Just take what I can get, and put it out of my head."

With a hand that trembled slightly, Mr. Webber

took a blue bandana from his back pocket and patted his bald head. "Mr. Smith, didn't you understand what was in all those papers that you just signed?"

"Well, maybe not *every*thing," Arnie confessed, "but I caught the general drift. The store belongs to me, free and clear. What I want to do now is sell it."

The lawyer smiled weakly. "I'm afraid it's not quite that simple. Do you recollect the papers," he asked cautiously, "that concerned themselves with mortgages, liens, taxes, cotton purchased, cotton sold . . . ?"

Arnie looked at him blankly. "Well, maybe not *them* things in particular."

Mr. Webber took a deep breath and tried again. "Do you recall some mention of accounts payable, accounts receivable, interest rates, credit charges . . . ?"

Arnie grinned sheepishly. "Not much, I guess. Is it important?"

The lawyer sat limply in his chair and rolled his eyes toward the ceiling. "Mr. Smith, would you like for me to give it to you in plain talk and save the legalities for later?"

"Yes, sir, I'd be much obliged if you did that."

The lawyer closed his eyes for a moment. "To begin with," he said slowly, "a store in the Southwest is more than just a building with goods for sale. It is a post office, a stage station, a meeting place, and sometimes it's even a church. It is an informal bank. It buys goods on credit and sells on credit. It makes loans, accepts notes, and sometimes it discounts the notes in order to obtain money to pay its own debts. It accepts produce in payment for goods it sells. A country store must necessarily become a speculator in commodities, a dealer in cotton, corn, and land, in order to stay in business."

Arnie's head was swimming. "I always figgered a store was a place where the owner tried to make a livin' by sellin' things for more than he paid for them, and that was all there was to it."

"A farmer," the lawyer told him, "could have told you different."

"Well," Arnie said wearily, "I don't ever aim to be a postmaster or banker or anything like that. All I want is to sell out. What do you figger she's worth?"

Webber thought about it. "In a good year maybe thirty thousand dollars."

Arnie was stunned. He had been thinking along the line of a few hundred at most. But thirty thousand dollars! He tried to think of it in terms that he could understand, in horses, or cattle, or silver-mounted saddles. In Stetson hats and handmade boots and old Kentucky whisky.

"In a good year," Webber repeated. "Right now times are hard."

"How much is she worth right now, hard times and all?"

"The value of land is down, and a big part of the store's assets are in land. So is the price of cotton and corn, and the store has a big stake in crops that won't even be grown for another year."

"How much?" Arnie pressed.

"Providing you could find a buyer . . . including accounts receivable . . . everything. Maybe three thousand dollars."

"I'll take it," Arnie said without hesitation. "Even less if I have to. Will you find me a buyer?"

"Until business improves, I don't think anybody could find you a buyer. And even if you found one, don't you see what it would mean?"

Arnie stared at him. "Long's I get my money, that's all I care about."

"Nevertheless . . ." Mr. Webber's smile was grim. "This is what would happen. The new owner would immediately call in all overdue notes and discount them at one of the Eastern banking houses. The farmers would be put off their land that some of them have been on since the Texas Revolution. At best a lot of people would go hungry if the store changed hands right now, and some of them might even starve."

Suddenly angry, Arnie lurched up from the chair. "Whose lawyer are you anyway? I come to you with a simple proposition to sell the store, and you accuse me of starvin' folks off their land."

Webber smiled a sad little smile and shrugged. "I

didn't mean to offend. I was just explaining the way things are nowadays . . ."

"I know," Arnie snorted. "Hard times. It's hard times with cowhands too. I ain't even got a saddle to put on a horse, if I had a horse. I ain't even got a decent pair of work pants, all I've got is that store. And I aim to sell it."

"Sit down, sit down," Mr. Webber said gently. "I was your uncle's lawyer for a long time, Mr. Smith, and I'll be yours for as long as you want me. I can see that you're persuaded to sell the store, so I'll do what I can to find you a buyer."

Arnie sank slowly back to the chair. After a moment he said sheepishly, "I guess 'hard times' has got to be a tender subject with me. I didn't aim to holler at you."

"That's all right. How would you like for me to go through these papers again and explain the points you don't understand?"

The prospect caused Arnie's head to throb, but he nodded resignedly. Apparently, getting the store off his hands wasn't going to be accomplished overnight. As long as it was his, he might as well know something about it.

CHAPTER FOUR

It was almost midnight when Herbert Webber wound up his patient lecture on the economics of back-country merchandising. Arnie was sure that he would never understand the cabalistic scribblings that went by the name of double-entry bookkeeping, but at least he was not quite as ignorant as he had been earlier. Webber drilled into him the importance of liens and promissory notes and interest rates. "The details you can leave to Purdy," the lawyer said, "until you get the hang of the books."

"This Purdy. Can he be trusted?"

Mr. Webber was clearly appalled at the implication that Harve Purdy might be other than completely trustworthy. "Your uncle trusted him for forty years."

"Then," Arnie said coolly, "I guess he'll do." He was thinking of the two sodbusters who had knocked him on the head. The experience had taught him one thing, at least. Arnie Smith was a stranger in a strange country, and he meant to keep a suspicious eye on it for as long as he remained here. Which, he devoutly hoped, would not be long.

Mrs. Webber had made him a pallet on the sleeping porch in back of the house. Arnie lay there for a long while, smoking thin brownpaper cigarettes and getting used to the fact of being a property owner. All the property he had ever wanted was a good horse and a decent rig, and here he was all of a sudden the owner of a dozen farms, and no telling how many bales of cotton that was stored somewhere waiting for higher prices—Arnie didn't even know where. And liens and notes and mortgages, he owned them too. All the work and sweat of the coming year—even before the sodbusters pulled a boll of cotton or shucked an ear of corn, they already owed it to Arnie Smith. The notion that other people were beholden to him for work that they hadn't even done yet gave him a queer feeling in the pit of his stomach. He decided that he didn't much like it.

Of course, he reminded himself, there were the debts of the store, the money that Smith General Mercantile Company owed to the wholesalers in Nashville and New Orleans and St. Louis and other places. They also belonged to Arnie Smith.

He thought about his uncle, working hard all his life to build up the business, and when he died all he had was an account of how much others owed to him and how much he owed to others. Had he ever got any enjoyment out of it? How many times had he ever gone to town and seen the elephant, as the saying went? How many girls with brassy laughter and soft caresses, like Brickyard McCarstairs, had he ever known? Not many, Arnie guessed. With that bleak thought in his mind, he went to sleep.

The next morning Arnie went to the office with Webber to wait for the stage. The through coach was due at the wagon yard, where it changed horses, at nine o'clock, the lawyer said. But it was usually late by an hour or so. Sometimes it was late a day or more, depending on the roads and the weather. "I got to thinkin' about my uncle last night," Arnie said. "Did you know him very well?"

"Hinkle, Mawson, and Sylvester, while the firm was still together, handled Mr. Smith's legal business for the best part of forty years. I knew him for about half that time."

"What kind of a man was he? That may sound like a queer question for me that was his nephew to be askin', but him and my pa never had much to do with each other."

Mr. Webber appeared to give the question considerable thought as they walked along. "He was a good businessman," he said at last. "He kept the store going where others would have failed."

Arnie waited for him to go on, but that was all Herbert Webber had to say on the subject on Syrus Smith.

Arnie wisely decided to let the subject drop.

The stagecoach, making its meandering way to Shreveport, Louisiana, was only an hour late that day. "Much obliged for everything," Arnie said, shaking hands with the lawyer.

"I'll start writing some letters, talk to some folks

I know. If there's a buyer for the store in this part of Texas, I'll find him."

Arnie grinned wistfully and climbed aboard. "I guess you know where to find me."

Now that he was on the last leg of the adventure he was anxious to get it over with. He wedged himself into the corner of the coach and watched the post oaks and small patches of farm land move by with deadly monotony. Once, at a particularly rough stretch of road when the coach slowed almost to a stop, Arnie hollered up to the driver, "I thought this was supposed to be piney wood country!"

"You thought wrong!" the driver hollered back.

Arnie was not particularly surprised, as the whimsey of men who made railroad maps was well known.

Because of the poor condition of the road the distance from Placer to Smith seemed much longer than the ten miles promised by Herbert Webber. Bored by the scenery, Arnie closed his eyes and dozed whenever the jolting of the coach would allow it. The driver jarred him out of one of these fitful naps by putting his head in the window and hollering, "This is Smith!"

Arnie sat up rubbing his eyes. The coach had pulled up on the hitching ground beneath a towering hackberry tree, at one end of the store building. Behind the hackberry tree was the inevitable well with its gallows-like pulley contraption and tin bailer. Behind the well was the store's equally inevitable lean-to shed room.

To Arnie's eyes the building itself was distressingly like any other country store in the Southwest. The same two stories, the square false front, the double front doors, the twin front windows barred with iron. The inevitable sign beside the front door declared in scaling black letters: "United States Post Office. Smith, Texas."

The area around the store yard was completely surrounded by thickets of scrub timber. Arnie could hear the sighing of the wind moving through leaved branches. There was a dry and dusty smell to the place. A single dilapidated wagon stood on the hitching ground in front of the store.

With some dismay Arnie climbed out of the coach. The driver got down a small mail sack and grinned at what he saw on Arnie's face. "Not much doin' on a weekday. She livens up some on Saturday."

As they walked across the store yard a man appeared in the doorway. "Here's your mail, Purdy," the driver told him, "and here's your new boss. You owe me a ticket for his trip up from Placer."

Harve Purdy was a thin, grim man who sported a green eyeshade on his bald head and black elastic garters on the sleeves of his hickory shirt. He came out to the porch and accepted the mail sack. "One of the clerks will write the ticket." He glanced sharply at Arnie. "You took your time about gettin' here."

"Well," Arnie started to explain, "Mr. Webber's letter got laid up in Dodge, and I was with a cow outfit down in the Cherokee . . ."

Purdy turned curtly in midsentence and returned to the dim interior of the store. Arnie stood for a moment, not knowing quite what to do. The stage driver got his ticket from the clerk and returned to his high seat. "Boy," he called quietly. When Arnie looked around he lowered his voice still further. "I guess it ain't none of my business, but if I was you I wouldn't expect a whole lot of help from old Purdy."

Arnie scowled. "Why not?"

"Because he's Purdy. That's reason enough." Then he wished he'd never spoken; he quickly released the brake and whipped the team out of the store yard.

With a sorrowful little groan, Arnie climbed the porch steps and went into the store. A big yellow cat uncurled on a stack of bolt goods and blinked at him with golden eyes. "Howdy, feller," Arnie grinned. He scratched the cat's ears.

At the right side of the store entrance Harve Purdy was sorting mail behind the barred postal window. Arnie sighed and went up to the window and said quietly, "We ain't goin' to get off on the wrong foot, are we, Mr. Purdy?"

A pair of sharp eyes shot him a narrow look from

beneath the green eyeshade. "I don't know what you're talkin' about."

"I'm sorry I didn't get here sooner. I'm sorry I missed my uncle's funeral—but I got here as soon as I could."

"It's none of my business. I'm just the book-keeper here."

"But you've been here a long time. The lawyer down at Placer says you was a big help to my uncle—I was hopin' you'd want to help me too."

Harve Purdy clamped his mouth shut and pigeon-holed a letter. "I do my job."

"All right," Arnie told him resignedly, "you can start by makin' me out a money order."

Mr. Purdy frowned disapprovingly. "Who would you be sendin' a money order to?"

Arnie had a powerful desire to see that thin, tightly locked mouth fall open in surprise. "Get your writin' pen," he said. When Purdy had reluctantly picked up his pen and opened a book of money order blanks, Arnie said, "Make it out for two dollars. It goes to Robert Wakefield Hefford, the Tennessee Repeating Firearms Company, Nashville, Tennessee."

Purdy's mouth did not fall open, but he did look shocked. "What do you know about Robert Wakefield Hefford?"

"I know I owe him two dollars and I aim to pay him."

With great reluctance, the bookkeeper filled out

the form and shoved it under the iron grating. "That'll be two dollars, on top of the money order fee. Two dollars and thirty cents."

Arnie grinned. "Bill the store for it."

Purdy looked as if he had been slapped. "I can't do that!"

"The store's good for two dollars and thirty cents, ain't it?"

Purdy sputtered. "Yes, but . . ."

"And I own the store, don't I? If there's any doubt in your head about that, I can show you the papers to prove it."

Purdy was an old man set in his ways. He didn't unbend easily. "Yes," he said grimly, "I think I'll just take a look a them papers. If you don't mind."

While the bookkeeper carefully read the legal transfer of store ownership, Arnie addressed an envelope to Hefford's company and shoved it back under the grill. "You can bill the store for postage too, while you're at it."

Purdy was an older and angrier man when he finished reading the legal document. "All right, *Mr. Smith*," he said with heavy sarcasm. "If you want to upset forty years of bookkeepin', that's your business."

"I'm glad we got that straightened out," Arnie told him with a strained grin. "It's my business." But even as he said it he realized that he was making a serious mistake, maybe a fatal one. Forty years of loyalty could not be brushed aside so easily. The right thing, he knew, would be to apologize immediately and try to get back on a proper footing.

But apologizing to a man like Harve Purdy was not an easy matter. There was so much hostility in those small, piercing eyes that Arnie's words stuck in his throat. By the time he thought of something to say, Purdy had slammed out of the tiny cubicle which was the United States Post Office of Smith, Texas, and stomped out of sight behind a forest of hanging harness leather.

Arnie chucked the yellow cat under its chin and said, "Well, to hell with him. What say we go back here and check up on the stock of sardines?"

The cat looked at him and yawned. Arnie picked up the animal and tucked it under his arm like a sack of feed and made his way between dry goods tables, stepping around tubs of onion sets and seed potatoes, the advertisements of spring, heading generally toward the big red wheel of a coffee grinder which he could just see over a mountain of gingham. All country stores were laid out to the same general pattern, and this one was no different. Where you saw the coffee grinder there would be a wheel of yellow cheese beside it. And shelves of sardines and salmon and cove oysters and canned tomatoes. Nearby would be a barrel for crackers and one for pickles and another for lard, and next to the wall would be a long covered bin, and that would be the "meat box" filled with faintly rancid sides of dry salt pork.

When Arnie reached the spot it was just as he had known it would be. At the end of the counter, beside the cheese, there was a cleared area known as the "lunch counter." Arnie put the cat on the floor and rummaged among the shelves, pulling down cans and parcels as he pleased. Standing beside the meat box was a gray, quiet, gently smiling man wearing a clerk's apron. He was so quiet and unobtrusive that Arnie didn't even see him until he had started laying out his lunch on the counter.

"Howdy," Arnie said, slightly on the defensive. "I ain't had anything to eat since breakfast. That was down at Placer this mornin'." He began opening a can of sardines. "I take it you're one of the clerks here."

"Lovin'," the man said. There was even a pleasant grayness in his voice. "Matt Lovin'. I'm the only regular clerk we got right now."

"Well, Matt, have you been here long?"

"Almost twenty years I was with Mr. Syrus." He gazed up at the hundred items hanging from the store rafters—the buggy harness, the bridles, the cheap shuck collars, the pots and pans. "I wouldn't mind too much about Mr. Purdy. He's had a heap on his mind since Mr. Syrus passed on."

Arnie dropped a sardine off the tip of his knife and the cat pounced on it and devoured it before it hit the floor. "I almost got the notion that Purdy figgered the store belonged to him. Is there any reason

79

you know about that he should think a thing like that?"

"No, sir. It's just that he's been here a long time, I guess." Arnie shoved sardines and crackers and cheese in his direction, but Matt Loving shook his head. "I bring my dinner with me when I come to work."

"Matt, do you happen to know anything about double-entry bookkeepin'?"

The clerk shook his head negatively. "No, sir. Don't nobody here know anything about that except Mr. Purdy."

They listened to the clanging of a hammer on metal in back of the store building. "Has the store got a regular blacksmith?" Arnie asked.

"Not regular. When work piles up Abe Cutter comes in for a day or so and helps out." Then, as if he had quietly read Arnie's mind, "I think that's where Mr. Purdy is now."

Without actually saying so, he was suggesting that it was time Arnie straightened out his relationship with the bookkeeper, before it was too late. Arnie grinned wearily. "Matt, you don't know of anybody that wants to buy a country store, do you?"

Clear alarm showed in the clerk's gray eyes. "Buy the store? No sir, I sure don't know anybody like that."

Arnie gave the rest of the sardines to the cat and went out to the brush arbor blacksmith shed that stood a short distance behind the store. Purdy wasn't there. Arnie went around to the front of the building and found him sitting stiffly on the end of the porch, gazing fiercely out at the thickets of the post oak.

"Mr. Purdy," Arnie said with all the patience he could summon, "I guess I spoke out of turn a while ago. I'd be much obliged if you would put that out of your head so's we can sort of start over from the first. The way I look at it, I need a bookkeeper and you need a place to work. We might as well make the best of a poor bargain, if that's what it is."

Purdy raised his head and glared at him from beneath his eyeshade. "This store belongs to me, by rights. Me and your uncle had an understandin'. When he passed on, everything was to go to me."

"That ain't what he said in his will."

"He lied. He cheated me out of what's rightly mine. All this time—forty years!—I worked day and night to keep the business from goin' under. Good times and bad, I was always on the job. Where was *you* all that time?"

"Well, about half the time I hadn't been born yet."

Purdy clamped and unclamped his bitter mouth. "Your uncle never even mentioned *havin'* any kin-folks. He lied about that too. Lettin' on all that time that the place would go to me."

"Mr. Purdy," Arnie said with sudden reckless-ness, "maybe my uncle did cheat you. I don't know about that. But I do know this store is legally mine, and I don't aim to let it go. I know you keep the books, and your work is important. If you was to quit, maybe the store would go bust—but if that's the way it's goin' to be, there ain't nothin' I can do to stop it. Because we're goin' to have an understandin', Mr. Purdy. Right now."

Purdy looked at him as if he were looking at a maniac. "What do you mean?"

"I mean I want to know right now whether you aim to go on workin' for me the way you worked for my uncle. If you don't, then you can draw your time. And that will be the end of it."

In Purdy's eyes a flicker of fear penetrated the glitter of anger. "This store wouldn't last a week, it wouldn't last no time at all, if I was to get up and quit!"

"That's somethin' we'll have to see about when the time comes. What about it, Mr. Purdy? Do you go on workin', or don't you?"

The bookkeeper's eyes darted from side to side, like a cornered animal searching for escape. He wet his thin lips with his tongue. "You don't know nothin' about runnin' a store. You got to have somebody to show you."

"You're right," Arnie told him placidly, "about not knowin' anything about storekeepin'. Until a few days ago I didn't even know there *was* a store. So if she goes bust, she goes bust—I never wanted to be a storekeeper anyway."

Purdy was appalled at the young man's reckless-
ness. Obviously, Arnie Smith was in no mood to be
bluffed or bullied; he was perfectly willing to let
the entire business collapse if he didn't get his way.
The bitter bookkeeper clenched his fists for a
moment. "All right," he said at last, getting shakily
to his feet. "I'll do my job."

Arnie beamed. He was not too proud of the way
he had to face the prospect of keeping the store's
books himself. "Fine," he said briskly, rubbing his
hands together and putting the moment of unpleasantness out of his mind. "Now, there must be a
place for me to bunk around here. My uncle had a
shack or somethin', didn't he?"

Purdy was already walking away, stiffly, angrily.
"Matt Lovin' will show you."

The friendly gray clerk took Arnie around to the
rear of the store and showed him the cramped lean-
to which was built like an afterthought against the
rear of the shed room. Arnie raised the door's
wooden latch and peered inside. "My uncle sure
wasn't a man for fall-de-rall and frills!"

Matt Loving smiled. "Mr. Syrus never spent
much time in this room, except to sleep, and sometimes to cook. In there, in the store, was his home,
I guess."

Arnie stepped cautiously into the gloom of that
windowless little shed. "There's a lamp next to the
bunk," Loving said. Arnie found the bunk by
cracking his shins on the rope-strung frame. He

struck a match and lit a coal oil lamp, and almost wished he hadn't.

"It ain't much, I guess," the clerk said apologetically.

"Well," Arnie admitted, "it sure ain't no 'big house' at some rich cowman's headquarters. But I guess it's better'n sleepin' in the weather." He inspected the plank-floored cubicle without enthusiasm. Besides the bunk there was a monkey stove with the stovepipe angling out through the side of the room. A scaling black oak wardrobe stood against the wall next to the shed room. Beside the door there was a shelf that served as a washstand, with the usual bucket and dipper and granite basin. For a man who had owned property worth thirty thousand dollars, it did seem that Syrus Smith could have built himself a better place to live.

"What I need worse than anything else," Arnie told Loving, "is to get out of these jeans and into some decent work clothes. Does the store carry a good grade of California pants?"

The clerk shook his head regretfully. "Levis is too expensive for folks hereabouts. Anyhow, we don't get many cowhands comin' through."

"Let's go back to the store and have a look," Arnie said with a hint of a sigh.

As Arnie reentered the store the realization suddenly struck him. *This is mine! It belongs to me!* He stood for several moments taking it in. The shuck collars hanging from the ceiling, the cheap enameled pots and pans, the hundreds of items of foodstuffs and medicines and notions. The furniture, the tools, the hundreds of yards of bolt goods. It all belonged to Arnie Smith!

He stood in the doorway looking and sniffing. Even the smell of the place was a heady sensation. The smell of leather, and wood, and mice, and green coffee and roasted coffee, and cheese, and pickles, and the sizing on the stacks of gingham and domestic, the starch in the sleazy hickory shirting, the smell of onion sets, and molasses, and coal oil and whisky—yes, whisky!—and of gun oil, and block salt, and the rancid fat of salt pork and lard, the tempting sweetness of stick candy, the man smell of chewing tobacco and sack tobacco and cheap cigars, and a hundred other mingled aromas that he could not at the moment give name to. He breathed it all in and for the first time understood a little of what it meant to be an owner of property.

"Ready-mades are upstairs," Matt Loving said, "if you want to look."

Arnie nodded and they climbed the wide stairway to the second floor. Harve Purdy was back in his post office cubicle writing something in a heavy ledger. He did not look up.

At the near end of the second floor there were racks of women's dresses and coats, shelves and tables of millinery material and corsets and hats and spool-heeled shoes and padded underthings that menfolk were careful not to stare at as they mounted the stairs. At the far end of the room there were plows and cultivators and planters, as well as hand tools. There were factory-made coffins with polished brass hardware, and cheaper unfinished coffins without hardware. And there were fixtures for those who could not afford a ready-made coffin—iron or brass handles, hinges, bolts of crinkled white and ivory-colored material for lining the boxes, and cross-shaped nails to hold it in place. And there were racks of men's suits and tables of folded pants and shirts. The shirts were invariably shapeless blouselike articles of striped hickory, the suits carelessly made of the cheapest jean material. Arnie groaned as he moved his hand over the rough wool-and-cotton pants.

"You could special order a pair of Levis from New Orleans," Matt Loving said doubtfully.

Arnie made a sound of resignation. "I can learn to wear jeans, I guess. For as long as I have to stay here." He selected a pair of lined pants, a hickory shirt, and a cheap wool hat that would immediately lose its shape the first time it got wet.

He hated the new shirt almost as much as the jean pants. The body was too big, the armholes too small, the tail too short. The garment seemed to have been made of unmatching and unrelated parts, except that it was all of the same shoddy material. But it was the best the store afforded, so he put it on and buttoned it up with the dim hope that it would set to his body with wearing.

He knew without asking that a country store in the post oaks would not stock the expensive boots that a cowhand considered necessary work equipment. He settled for a pair of red top button shoes only slightly more comfortable than the shapeless brogans he now wore. "Lord help me," he complained, "if anybody I know comes through and sees me in a rig like this!"

Matt Loving was standing by looking vaguely uneasy. In his hand was a sales book and from time to time he would write something in it. Suddenly he shoved the book at Arnie. "Would you mind puttin' your name on this, Mr. Smith?"

Arnie took the book and scowled at it. It was a bill not only for his new clothing but for the sardines and crackers that he and the yellow cat had eaten earlier. "Matt," he said patiently, "there's somethin' you don't seem to understand. These things belong to me now. The store belongs to me."

"I know, but Mr. Purdy'll want this so's he can add the things to your account."

"I don't want an account. I don't want to be charged for things I already own."

The clerk spread his hands helplessly, and Arnie sensed that this was the beginning of an argument he had no chance of winning. He signed the sales ticket, and Loving went downstairs to turn it over to Purdy.

Arnie browsed for a while among the clutter of the upstairs room making a halfhearted attempt to familiarize himself with some of the stock. On the wall, above the stack of factory-made coffins, was a small framed document that declared this room to be the official meeting place for the Placer County lodge of the Woodmen of the World. Beside it was another framed paper making the same claim for the Masons. Self-consciously, he wandered through the women's section of the room, noting with some embarrassment the stacks of bustles, false breasts, corsets, stocking holders, ladies' hats, fancy cloth, toilet soap, pomades, various herb mixtures recommended for "female complaints," camphor, asafetida, black rubber nursing nipples. With his face burning, Arnie fled that part of the room and returned to the ground floor.

A black field hand was standing in the shadows, motionless, almost invisible, while Matt Loving busily got together an order for his boss. Arnie went to the heavy heart-pine counter where the order lay. It was written in pencil on a piece of brown wrapping paper. *Dear Mister Purdy please hand Ralph the followin things if you got them and put it on my bill five pounds of dry salt meat with some lean in it if you got it. 10 pounds flour not the best but gud enuf for bakin and a handle for my plow and one gal onion sets also a middlin bottle morphine for Delly as she is feelin poorly and Ill settl up soon as my cottons in.* It was signed *Fred Medder.*

"What's wrong with Missus Medder," Arnie asked, "that she needs a bottle of morphine?"

The clerk's expression turned curiously blank. "Life's hard in the post oaks, especially on women and mules—maybe a little dram of morphine now and again makes it look a little better." He cut off a piece of fat meat and put it on the scales—it weighed slightly less than three pounds. He put it with the rest of the order.

Arnie scowled. "This note of Medder's says he wants five pounds of meat."

The clerk smiled in his quiet way. "I know what he wants, but his credit is worth only three pounds. And five pounds of flour, not ten. But he can have the handle for his plow and the onion sets."

"And the morphine?"

Loving nodded sadly. "And the morphine. Delly Medder couldn't do without that."

"Just who is it," Arnie asked in a puzzled, slightly angry tone, "that decides that a family gets five pounds of flour instead of the ten they want. How do you know they ain't goin' to go hungry?"

"The fact is," Loving admitted, "I'm afraid the Medders will go hungry, for a little while anyway, until next month when they're good for another order. As for who does the decidin', it used to be Mr. Syrus. Since Mr. Syrus was took from us, it's been Mr. Purdy. Now, after you've had the chance to get to know folks, I guess the job will fall to you."

"Well," Arnie said coldly, "I sure don't think much of an outfit that lets folks go hungry when it ain't necessary."

Again the clerk flashed his quiet smile. "Sometimes I think the same thing. But then I think, 'Five pounds of flour and three pounds of fat meat is better'n nothin'.' And that's what it would soon be, if somebody didn't hold the credit down. Nothin'. Because the store would soon go bust."

The field hand left with his pitifully small parcel of foodstuffs, and his plow handle and his onion sets. And the morphine for Mrs. Medder. Arnie stood in front of the store for a while feeling depressed. What he needed was the company of cowhands. Long on laughter and good times, short on worries and cares. There in the oppressive atmosphere of this small country store, it was easy to forget the hard life that the working cowhand led. The long hours in the saddle, bad food, sleeping in the rain, stampedes.

A farm wagon rattled up in the store yard. A sod-buster, white-faced, with panic in his eyes, scrambled out of the wagon and pounded up the steps to the store. "Purdy, I got to have the madstone in a hurry! My youngest son's been bit by a mad dog!"

Purdy, still in the post office cubicle, heard the man's excited message without blinking an eye. He pulled down an account book, turned a few pages, then looked through the barred window at the farmer. "You're already over the limit for this month, Aram. Have you got a dollar cash money for the rent of the madstone?"

Arnie stared for a moment, unable to believe that

he had heard correctly. He went up to the grilled window. "Do you want to tell me that this store's got a madstone and charges folks for the use of it?"

"That's right," the bookkeeper said coolly. "A madstone's like medicine, and anybody'll tell you that medicine don't come free." He turned to the farmer. "You've got a dollar put by for a special time, haven't you, Aram? Well, this is that special time. You just hand me the dollar and Matt will get you the madstone."

Arnie, in a choked voice, said, "To hell with the dollar! Get him the madstone, Purdy."

The bookkeeper looked at Arnie in amazement. "He's got the money. It'll take him a while to conclude that he's got to dig it up. But dig it up he will, you just give him a little time."

This time Arnie spoke in hot anger. "For the sake of a dollar you'd take a chance on a boy's life? Goddamn you, Purdy, give him the madstone!"

The bookkeeper's face went white. He unclamped his jaws with difficulty and spoke harshly. "It's your store, Mr. Smith. If you're bound and determined to throw away money, that's your business." He nodded to the clerk. "Open the safe, Matt. Give Mr. Aram Plott the madstone and I'll put it on his bill."

This time Arnie lost his temper completely. "God damn it, Purdy, I said *give* him the madstone. I don't aim for this store to charge money for a thing that might save a boy's life."

The bookkeeper's face was set like rock. He pointed to a crowded shelf on the far wall. "See that shelf over there? It's medicine, all medicine. Maybe two, three hundred dollars' worth of it. Do you aim to give that away, too?"

Arnie hesitated, but only for an instant. "If the man didn't have the money to pay for it, I would."

"And over there in the bin underneath the shelf are some trusses. They cost the store maybe twenty dollars. If a man come in and says he's got a rupture and wants a truss but he ain't got any money, are you goin' to *give* him one free of charge?"

"That's different," Arnie hedged. "Ruptures don't kill a man."

"Yes they do," Purdy said coldly. "Sometimes."

"Then I'd give him the truss."

"And you'd be a fool," the bookkeeper snapped. He slammed the heavy account book shut and stumped out of the store.

When the farmer was gone and they could no longer hear the rattling of his wagon, Arnie and Matt Loving stood near the front of the store in silence. Arnie had the uneasy feeling that he had done something very wrong, but he couldn't think what it was. If a similar situation came up, he would do the same thing again, antagonizing Purdy and very likely setting a precedent that could doom the store in the future. At last he turned to the clerk and asked wearily, "Did I do wrong?"

"To Mr. Purdy's way of thinkin', you did. Aram

Plott is a close-fisted man and a middlin' farmer—most likely he had the money put by, just like Mr. Purdy said. Of course you couldn't of knowed that."

"Even if he'd of come with the money in his hand, I couldn't charge a man for usin' a madstone. I never even heard of such a thing."

Matt Loving sighed and smiled his sad smile. "I don't know. Maybe nowadays we look at things different here in the post oaks. It's . . ."

"I know," Arnie broke in sourly. "It's hard times. The crazy thing about it is, that madstone is worthless. There never was a man that got cured of a mad dog bite by rubbing a stone on it. I've heard regular doctors say so."

The clerk gazed placidly out at the monotonous thickets of scrub timber. "It came from the belly of a white deer—or that's what Mr. Syrus always claimed anyhow. It's been in the store for more'n twenty years. A lot of folks have used it."

"Did it cure them?"

"Some of them," Loving shrugged. "Or it seemed to."

"Ah hell!" Arnie said, throwing his arms in the air in frustration. "I wish they'd never let me out of the jailhouse in Dodge!"

CHAPTER FIVE

The next morning Arnie was in the shed room plugging a leak in the coal oil barrel when Matt Loving came in. "Mr. Purdy wants to see you."

"What about?"

"I guess it's about Lon Fuller. Lon's a tenant farmer, works a little patch of corn and cotton on shares with Fred Medder."

"What has Lon Fuller got to do with me?"

The clerk shrugged. "He claims his wife's down with the spring fever. Wants a bottle of Plantation Bitters to perk her up. Trouble is, he ain't got any money, and he's out of credit. He heard that you let the madstone out free to Aram Plott, so he figgered you wouldn't mind doin' the same for him with a bottle of bitters."

"Can't Mr. Purdy handle it?"

"He can give Lon the bitters, but he says it has to be accounted for, one way or another, in the books. He wants your name on the sales ticket."

Arnie straightened up and looked at Loving. "Maybe. I don't know. How much does the bitters cost us?"

"Little less than twenty cents a bottle, bought by the case."

"What do we sell it for?"

"Fifty cents."

It seemed to Arnie that a lot was being made over

a twenty-cent bottle of medicine. "How long has Lon Fuller been a customer here?"

"Off and on maybe a dozen years."

"Then give him the bitters and put it on his bill." The clerk nodded but didn't look happy about it. "Well," Arnie demanded, "what are you lookin' so long-faced about?"

"Mr. Purdy'll still want your name on Lon's ticket. Next month he's goin' to be fifty cents short of credit—that's got to be accounted for in the books."

Arnie groaned in irritation. "Tell you the truth, Lovin', I'm beginnin' to get a little sick of them books of Purdy's." But he went up front and signed the ticket anyway. There was a grim, smug look on Purdy's face when he transferred the amount on the ticket to one of the big leatherbound books.

Early that afternoon a field hand appeared with a note from his landlord. *My woman hears from Aram Plott's wife that your givin away free medicine to thems sick. This is my hand Elmore let him have one Wine of Cardui, two Jones Mountain Herbs and one big bottle King's New Discovery. Dont put it on my bill its for Elmores family as theyre all down with the complaint.*

Purdy flashed a small, vicious grin as he handed the order to Arnie. "I tried to tell you you was startin' somethin' when you gave Aram Plott the use of that madstone."

Arnie looked at the field hand who was standing

just inside the doorway grinning expectantly. Then he carefully read the farmer's note and was outraged. "What in damnation's this all about?"

Matt Loving said quietly, "I guess Lon Fuller told somebody about the bitters. And they told Fred Medder, and Fred told somebody else. . . . News travels fast in the post oaks, especially when it's somethin' bein' given away."

"Hell," Arnie bawled, "I don't even *know* this man. I don't know that his family is sick, or that he's even *got* a family. And even if he's got one and they are sick, what would he do with *three* bottles of medicine?"

"Four," the clerk smiled gently. "Well, for one thing these bitters is mostly alcohol, and a good deal cheaper than whisky."

Arnie nodded grimly. "I see. So that's the way it goes when a man tries to do the decent thing. They take advantage."

Loving sighed resignedly. "I'm afraid that's the way it is."

"Well, to hell with them. I ain't givin' away any more medicine."

"Folks won't like it, givin' it to Lon Fuller and Aram Plott and not to them."

"If they don't like it, let them take their business to one of the stores in Placer." To the field hand he said, "Go back and tell your boss that we ain't givin' away any more medicine. We ain't givin' away nothin' at all. You savvy?"

The hand's grin faded. He left the store long-faced, grumbling to himself. In a mood of profound disgust, Arnie tramped to the rear of the store and drew himself a dram of Maryland Bourbon from a twenty-gallon keg and downed it at one gulp.

But Purdy and Loving managed to remove the pleasure from such a simple act as taking a drink of his own whisky. The clerk silently recorded the unprofitable act on a sales slip. In due time Purdy would transfer it to his books.

That night Arnie laboriously composed a letter to Herbert Webber in Placer. . . . *I sinsirily hope that you have rounded up a buyer for this store by the time this letter reches you as I have definitely concluded that storekeepin aint my line never mind the profit all I want is enough for a decent horse and rig. . . .*

Two days later a reply arrived from Placer on the northbound stage. . . . *Please believe me when I say that I do appreciate your desire to profitably dispose of the Smith General Mercantile Company. However, due to the economic situation back East, as well as in our own area . . . necessary to have patience . . . in time I feel everything will work to our advantage, but . . . cash in short supply . . . be assured that I am doing everything possible . . .*

In disgust, Arnie balled the letter and hurled it to the floor. "For the price of a cheap pistol and a dollar watch," he told the yellow cat, "I'd get up and leave this store right where she sets and head back to cow country."

The cat looked at him uninterestedly and yawned.

The next day was Saturday. Arnie, from his sagging bunk in his lean-to shed behind the store, heard Harve Purdy opening the doors a good hour earlier than usual. Within a matter of minutes he heard the sound of hoofs rounding the corner of the store building. That would be Abe Cutter, the blacksmith. Abe was also an hour earlier than normal.

By the time Arnie had dragged himself out of the bunk and splashed his face at the washstand, dawn was just starting to break through the post oaks. Matt Loving arrived as he always did, on foot, bringing his biscuit and meat lunch with him. He smiled at Arnie and said, "Long day today."

By nightfall Arnie would know what he meant.

He built a fire in the monkey stove and boiled ready ground coffee from the store. Coffee that Harve Purdy had duly charged him for, Arnie was sure. With a certain expertise that came from years of doing his own cooking in line camp shacks, he made his breakfast of side meat and flapjacks and wolfed it down.

He stepped outside and practiced breathing before entering the store. It was a warm spring morning with a taste of dust in the air—Arnie was not looking forward to the day ahead with much enthusiasm.

Inside the store a red-haired, red-faced young man about Arnie's age was behind a counter sorting brogans in the shoe bin. "This here's Patty Doul," Matt Loving said. "He helps out on Saturdays and at special times of the year, such as Christmas. Patty, shake hands with the new owner of the store."

Arnie shook hands with the grinning young Irishman and later said to Loving, "Does the store need another hand? It don't seem like we've got enough customers to carry another name on the payroll."

"The day ain't over yet," Loving said, and smiled mysteriously.

Arnie wandered about the store blowing out coal oil lanterns as full daylight broke on the timbered hills. He poked listlessly from shelf to shelf, table to table, telling himself that he was getting to know the stock. For a while he blundered idly about in the back half of the store where the heavy barreled goods and hardware were kept. The large barrel of raw corn whisky and the smaller keg of Maryland Bourbon. Strange—with all that whisky in the store, whisky legally his, he hadn't taken more than a couple of sips since he had been here. What was the fun of drinking whisky with storekeepers and sodbusters?

He meandered through the stocks of vinegar,

rice, coffee, salt, lard, molasses. He cut off a piece of yellow cheese as he passed the "lunch counter," ate part of it and gave the rest to the yellow cat that padded silently at his heels. What was the use of owning a store if you couldn't help yourself when you felt like it?

He pulled up a much-mended and wired-up cane-bottom chair and sat beside the cold potbellied stove and smoked a cigarette. Everybody else seemed to be busy; Patty Doul at the shoe bin, Loving with broom in the shed room, Purdy with his everlasting books. Only Arnie Smith could find nothing to do. The trouble with a country store was, no matter what you did to it, it always looked the same.

Still, even the owner felt guilty after a while, with so much activity all around him. He got to his feet and wandered up the stairway to the second floor.

"Good mornin'."

Arnie was startled to see a smiling young woman busily engaged in sorting stacks of corsets, shirt-waists, stocking holders, and bustles. "Good mornin'," he said from a respectful distance. He had studied the matter at some length and had decided that it was not proper for a man to pass closer than three or four feet to the female goods table if he could help it. "I didn't aim to come bustin' in on you. I didn't know anybody was up here."

She held a padded bust up to the light and dusted

it with a bunch of turkey feathers. "I'm Amy Hall. Didn't Mr. Purdy tell you?"

Arnie shook his head. "No, ma'am, he didn't."

"I work extra on Saturdays and holidays." She turned her smile on him and Arnie was dazzled. "That's about the only time womenfolks get to come to the store. I reckon you're Mr. Smith."

"Well," Arnie confessed, "I'm Arnie Smith, all right, ma'am."

"I was well acquainted with your uncle. He was a good man . . . in his way. An important man here in the post oaks."

Arnie didn't quite know what to say to that. Her favorable appraisal of his uncle, and then the qualification, had thrown him off balance. Suddenly he felt even more awkward than usual in his poor jean pants and ready-made shirt and ridiculous red top shoes. "Well, ma'am," he said at last, "I'm right proud to meet you."

She looked at him brightly as he backed off toward the stairway. He was afraid that she was going to laugh, but she didn't.

"Why in damnation didn't you tell me there was a woman in the place?" he demanded of Purdy when he got back downstairs.

The bookkeeper shot him a narrow look tainted with bitterness. "I wasn't sure you was all that interested in the business."

"It's my store. I got a right to know who's workin' for me." It occurred to Arnie that he was

101

continually having to remind people that this was his store, and it was a practice that he was beginning to get tired of.

Harve Purdy put down his pen and closed a heavy ledger. "Her name's Amy Hall. Her folks own their own place down south a piece, but to be truthful about it, Andrew Hall ain't no great shakes as a farmer. Which is why Amy clerks here whenever she gets the chance. In the wintertime, between harvest and plantin', she teaches school at Oak College."

"Oak College?"

"That's the schoolhouse between here and Placer."

Arnie was fairly stunned by this sudden flood of information from the close-mouthed bookkeeper. "Does the store really need two extra clerks on Saturdays?"

"Your uncle always kept two extra clerks on Saturdays. Syrus was a shrewd businessman; he wouldn't of paid out the money if it hadn't been necessary."

The first wagon arrived on the hitching ground shortly before midmorning. Arnie heard the ungreased wheels screaming long before the vehicle lurched into sight on the deep-rutted road.

"That's Croy Mackerson's outfit," said Matt Loving, who had moved his restless broom out to the front porch. "Always the first to get here, last to leave. I don't know why they bother. Their credit's down to six dollars a week—you wouldn't think it would be worth hitchin' up the team for."

Evidently the Mackersons thought differently. In the rickety farm wagon there were Croy Mackerson, his wife Flower, their six children in stairstep sizes, Flower's father, who was almost blind but never missed a Saturday trip to the store, and Croy's mother, who was reputed to be ninety-seven years old and traveled in royal style in her favorite rocker. The children spilled over the sides and scattered in all directions as soon as the wagon rattled to a stop. The womenfolks kept their seats, waiting for other farm families to arrive. Croy and his father-in-law brushed themselves off and hurried across the store yard as if on a matter of great urgency.

"Howdy, Croy. Howdy, Mr. King," Matt Loving said in his naturally courtly tone.

"Howdy, Matt," Mr. Mackerson said, then quickly lowered his voice to a conspiratorial level. "Is Mr. Purdy in the store now?"

"He's behind the post office window, I think, Croy."

The farmer nodded knowingly. "I knowed he'd be. That's the reason we got a early start this mornin'. I wanted to talk to old Purdy before ever'-body else started on him." His voice dropped still lower. "You think there's a chance I might get my credit raised, Matt?"

"Well, I don't know," the clerk told him. "This here's the man you'll have to talk to about that, Croy." He smiled quietly in Arnie's direction. "This here's Mr. Syrus's nephew, Arnie Smith. Mr. Smith's the owner of the store, now that his uncle's passed on."

The idea that this fair-cheeked young man might be a person of such importance seemed to be almost more than Croy Mackerson could accept. He stared at Arnie, his eyes bugging slightly. Even the almost-blind Mr. King stared at him, blinking his pale eyes rapidly.

"I'm proud to know you, Mr. Mackerson," Arnie said quickly, for he had the uneasy feeling that both men were about to start begging him for more credit. And he was learning, slowly, that credit was not a simple thing. "I'm new to the business," he rushed on before they could speak. "Mr. Purdy's still in charge of credit. You and Mr. King go right on in and talk to him."

When the farmers were inside, Loving glanced at Arnie with some amusement. "You know what I think? I think if they'd asked you for more credit, you'd of give it to them."

"Would that of been so bad?"

"Croy Mackerson's a good man—and the worst farmer in Placer County. His note's a year overdue, his crop this year don't stand a chance of coverin' his debts. Before next spring he'll lose his farm."

"Who to? The store?"

The clerk shrugged. "Unless you want to discount his note at one of the Eastern banking houses."

In the time Arnie had been here he had heard a great deal about credit and mortgages and interest rates and lien laws, but most of all about credit. He had a dim notion of the way it worked in eastern Texas. First, the merchant sized up his customer and made a mental judgment as to his willingness to work and pay his bills. Then he rode out and looked at the farm—other things being equal, a piece of bottom land would be worth a great deal more than a place on the side of a hill. Sometimes he would pick up some of the dirt and taste it on his tongue.

Then he would make a guess about the weather to come. Hot or cold. Wet or dry. It would all enter into the final calculations which decided how much credit the farmer would get for the year. If a plague of grasshoppers had been reported in Kansas, that would enter into it too. It might raise the price of corn in Texas, or the grasshoppers might move on south and wipe out the crop. It was for the merchant to decide.

When all calculations had been made a figure was applied to the farmer's account. In Croy Mackerson's case the figure, in good times, had been six hundred dollars. Fifty dollars a month, less credit charges and interest, was what Croy was worth on the books of the Smith General

Mercantile Company. In good times. In hard times the figure was cut in half.

At the moment Croy was worth twenty-five dollars a month. He could use it to buy anything the store stocked, from buggy whips to Maryland Bourbon, from stage tickets to postage stamps. If he wanted to buy something out of a mail order catalogue, he could do that too, and the store would make an added profit on the sale of the money order. But when the twenty-five dollars was used up, his credit was shut off until the next month. That was the way it worked at most country stores.

Arnie had known all of this in a vague sort of way, even before he had inherited the store, but he had never actually known a man like Croy Mackerson, who had to feed four adults and six children—never mind the livestock—on twenty-five dollars a month.

It seemed that Matt Loving had been watching the thoughts slowly turning in the new store owner's mind. He said, "Whatever you might hear about your uncle, Mr. Syrus was a fair man. Fair as a storekeeper can be, anyhow. It's only good business to give a man all the credit he can pay for—and sometimes Mr. Syrus gave more than that."

Arnie went back into the store and faced Purdy through the grilled window. "Did Mackerson talk to you about gettin' more credit?"

The bookkeeper's mouth pulled down as though he had bitten into a green persimmon. "He did. I told him he wasn't worth the twenty-five he's gettin'. Which is the truth. It ought to be cut to fifteen."

Arnie said, "Leave it like it is. Tomorrow I'll ride out and look at the farm."

The second wagon arrived on the hitching ground shortly before ten o'clock. The menfolks gathered with Croy Mackerson and Mr. King at one end of the store porch and began to talk. The womenfolks met at the Mackerson wagon. Another Saturday at Smith's store was officially under way.

By ten-thirty there were eighteen wagons on the hitching ground. By noontime there were thirty. Arnie came out of the almost empty store and was startled to see all the wagons and animals fanned out like the rear columns of a cavalry regiment. He guessed there were almost a hundred adults gathered in loose clusters at either end of the porch and at the blacksmith shed in back, or hunkered down in the shade of the big hackberry tree. From time to time the glassy glint of a fruit jar would flash in the sun as the men passed around the small containers of corn whisky.

The red-faced clerk, Patty Doul, came out to the porch and smoked a cigarette beside Arnie. Arnie asked, "How much whisky has the store sold this mornin'?"

"Not much. Maybe a quart or so."

"Seems like half the men out there have got a bottle in their pocket, or a jar where they can lay hands on it. Where do they get it?"

The clerk grinned. "Make it themselves, most of them. Not much call for store whisky, except at Christmas time. Any farmer worth his seed cotton wants a little bourbon in the house then."

Arnie shook his head in wonder. "I never knowed there was so many sodbusters in the whole county. Is that all they do on a Saturday, stand around and talk?"

"Things lively up as the day goes on. Once we had to call the sheriff's deputy from Placer. By the time he got here, of course, the trouble was over."

Arnie squinted. "What kind of trouble?"

"As I recollect, it was the Carbads and the Witters. They got into a cuttin' scrape over somethin', I forget what, and when it was over Jeff Carbad was dead, and Herb Witter was cut to the holler and died sometime the next day."

"Do you get trouble like that very often?"

Patty scratched his freckled nose. "Sometimes worse. But the families try to keep it quiet. The law in Placer don't hardly count up here in the post oaks. Families hereabouts settle things amongst theirselves."

"If somebody *does* get hurt, where would a body go to find a doctor?"

Apparently this was an entirely new and somewhat foolish idea, as far as the young clerk was concerned. "The only doc I know about is old McPhitter in Placer, and if he ever got hisself as far north as Smith, I never heard about it." He spat his burnt-out cigarette into the store yard. "I better get back in the store. There'll be a little lunch business, for them that can afford it. But the big rush will come later."

A short time later Arnie counted almost forty wagons on the hitching ground. Children and dogs swarmed about the store yard, the adults still gathered in prim little knots talking, talking. At last Arnie demanded of Matt Loving, "What in hell are they talkin' about anyhow?"

Loving smiled. "Politics, religion, weather, crops. The bank panic back East, the price of cotton. That's the men. Lord knows what the women talk about, but they never seem to explain. Farmin's a lonesome business, and hard. The work breaks your back, and your spirit. The soil gets a little poorer every year. You'll have to see it to know about it."

"I aim to do that," Arnie said. "I want to ride out to Croy Mackerson's and see if the store can give him more credit."

Some women came inside and skittered like faded shadows up the stairway. "That might be a good notion," Loving told him. "Mr. Syrus used to ride out every Sunday when the weather allowed, lookin' at the crops. Do you know much about cotton and corn?"

Arnie shook his head. "Not much."

"You'd better take somebody with you then. I'd

be proud to go, but I've got the service at Oak College in the mornin'."

"The service?"

Matt Loving laughed. "I thought you knew. On Sundays I'm the preacher at the schoolhouse— except for the summer when everybody's pickin' cotton."

By midafternoon the store was fairly crowded with women. Menfolks sometimes got to come to the store on a weekday; never the women. This was the only chance they had to see what was new, to ask the price of cotton cloth, or shyly caress a silk ribbon. They gazed longingly at the display of colognes—Hoyt's, American Girl, Duchess Ladies, Home Sweet Home—tiny bottles of magic that only a few of them could afford at twenty-five cents. Or amber combs set with glittering stones. Or hard leather shoes with daring spool heels and gleaming buttons. Or the cakes of colored and perfumed soaps: Pears, Wild Rose, Lenox, Dandelion, White Clover, magic names, far beyond the reach of most of them.

Before long a few farm women and younger sons of farm families began coming in with slips of paper on which were written out the "rations" for the coming week. Salt, flour, meat, calomel, coal oil. Rarely did the menfolks bring in an order themselves, unless they meant to settle their bill or ask for more credit. Within a matter of minutes the clerks, Harve Purdy included, were busily filling orders and placing the parcels outside on the porch where they could be easily loaded.

Arnie pitched in with Patty Doul at the meat box, cutting the slabs of fat pork and weighing it up for the senior clerks. "Why," he asked in irritation, "do they all wait till the last minute?"

"Lord knows," Doul grinned. "But they always do."

Arnie's hands and arms were soon slick with rancid pork fat. "This ain't no kind of work for a cowhand," he complained bitterly. "Sooner I was diggin' postholes for a cow outfit, or greasin' windmills. If anybody had of told me that Arnie Smith would get hisself caught clerkin' in a country store, sellin' dry salt meat to a bunch of sodbusters . . ."

Suddenly the activity in the store seemed to freeze. Arnie looked up, scowling, his heavy butcher knife cut halfway through a side of pork. Purdy, who had been counting out shotgun shells at the gun case, shot a look at Patty Doul. "Patty, get yourself over to the medicine shelf and clean it out!"

"What's goin' on here?" Arnie wanted to know.

"It's Sam Tillman!" the young clerk hissed from the side of his mouth. Quickly, he wiped his greasy hands on the legs of his jean pants. "Just stand steady. Most likely ever'thing will be all right." He started moving away from the meat box, making for the medicine shelves on the far wall.

A hatless farmer stood in the doorway, and there was an unmistakable wildness about him that caused Arnie to groan to himself. A drunk sodbuster! Well, it was no more than to be expected, the way corn whisky had been passing from hand to hand in the store yard. Arnie reached for a rag and wiped his hands. "Mr. Tillman? Is there somethin' I can do for you?"

It stood to reason that, cowhand or sodbuster, a drunk was a drunk. You talked to him quiet and gentle, hoping he wouldn't start busting up the place. Then you led him outside and turned him over to his friends. But Purdy shot Arnie an angry look when he started away from the meat box. "Stay where you are!"

"He's drunk; anybody can see that. I don't want him in the store."

"He ain't drunk. Just do like I say and don't move."

There was an urgency in Purdy's tone that Arnie had never heard before. He pulled up short. The store was perfectly silent except for the wheezing sound of Sam Tillman's breathing. Matt Loving, with a scoop of green coffee in his hand, stood like a wooden Indian in the back of the store. Only Patty Doul moved, and he very gingerly, as he rounded the thread counter, making for the far wall.

"If he ain't drunk, what is he?" Arnie asked.

The sodbuster turned toward him and fixed him for a moment with wild eyes. Then he started through the store, moving blindly, carrying his clenched fists at his sides like clubs. He pushed over a sack of seed potatoes. Then he brushed a counter and knocked over a display of lamp chimneys—the sound of shattering glass was startling and unnerving. He moved on through the store, making generally for the medicine shelf.

"Somebody's got to stop him," Arnie announced angrily, "before he busts everything in the place!" But stopping Sam Tillman was not likely to be an easy matter. He was a thick, heavy man with powerful shoulders and long, swinging arms. Arnie threw down his rag and reached for a display of hoe handles.

"Don't be a fool!" the bookkeeper snapped.

"I don't aim to have no drunk sodbuster bustin' up my store!" He moved up the aisle between rows of goods tables. "Tillman, we don't want no trouble here. Go back to the yard and talk to your pals."

The farmer stared at him with hot eyes. Arnie raised the hoe handle. "I don't want to hurt you, Tillman!"

The farmer came toward him looking as powerful as a locomotive. He crowded Arnie against a goods table, and Arnie, with a little groan of resignation, swung with the hoe handle.

The oak stick snapped over Tillman's head and the farmer didn't even blink. With a jerky swing of his arm he knocked Arnie onto a stack of hickory shorts, and the overturned table crashed to the floor. Tillman moved on steadily, powerfully, like a runaway freighter going downhill. "Purdy!" Arnie shouted to the bookkeeper, who was standing directly in front of the firearms case, "Get a gun! Stop him!"

The bookkeeper didn't move. He didn't even glance in Arnie's direction. Arnie pulled himself to his feet and threw himself at the sodbuster. Tillman knocked him down again. While all this was happening, Matt Loving stood perfectly still with the scoop of coffee in his hand. Purdy looked sour and angry but resigned to what would happen. Patty Doul had made it to the medicine shelf and was busily pulling down bottles of morphine, and the tiny one-ounce bottles of laudanum, as well as the small paper packages of gum and powdered opium.

Tillman saw what the clerk was doing and suddenly he threw up his hands and howled. It was a wild, animal sound that brought out the sweat on Arnie's neck. In an instant the farmer was blundering crazily over and through stacks of merchandise. He reached the medicine shelf and knocked Doul to the floor. Ignoring the morphine and opium, he pawed several of the small bottles of laudanum off the shelf and stuffed them in his pocket. In a frenzy he cracked one of the tiny bottles on the counter and licked liquid and broken glass out of the palm of his hand.

At last Tillman began backing away from the

wall, edging his way toward the front of the store. Arnie hollered again at the bookkeeper. "Get a gun and stop him, Purdy!"

"I ain't a gunfighter," Purdy said coldly. "Anyhow, he'll kill anybody that gets in his way, so don't aggravate him."

The big farmer slid through the doorway, leaving the store a shambles. Matt Loving put down his scoop of coffee and hurried to the front of the store in time to cut Arnie off.

"Don't try to catch him. Just leave him alone. There's nothin' to be done . . . nothin' at all!"

Arnie stared, outraged at the wreckage and furious at the clerks for having allowed it to happen. "What kind of men are you, without backbone or guts!" He bulled his way to the gun case and quickly took out a single-barrel shotgun—the one weapon in the case that was always kept loaded. Angrily, he shoved Loving to one side and ran to the porch.

That was as far as he got. Twenty or thirty farmers had suddenly congregated in front of the store's double doorway. They stood there like a living wall, barring Arnie's way. Arnie butted into them, but the wall of farmers would not move. He raised the shotgun and pointed it at them. "By God, if I have to shoot somebody to catch that store wrecker, why I'll do it!"

The wall did not budge. Over their heads Arnie could see Tillman stumbling blindly across the store yard, sucking on one of the tiny bottles of laudanum. Weaving drunkenly through the maze of wagons and teams, he disappeared into a stand of timber.

At last Arnie lowered the shotgun. His hands were sweating. In the pit of his stomach there was a quivering sickness. *"Lord,"* he thought wearily, *"what kind of people are these? What kind of a place is this?"*

Back in the store, Loving and Doul and Purdy were setting tables upright and picking up merchandise. They moved with the practiced rhythm of men who had done the same thing many times before.

Arnie put the loaded gun away. "Does this kind of thing happen often?" he asked shakily.

Patty Doul evened a stack of shirts like a gambler blocking a deck of cards. "Often enough."

"What was wrong with him? Is he a hophead?"

"Laudanum drinker," the young clerk said. "You never seen one of them before?"

"No."

Amy Hall had come down from the second floor at the start of the ruckus and now stood white-faced and trembling on the bottom landing. Matt Loving straightened up with an armful of bolt goods and smiled at her in his quiet way. "It's all over now, Miss Amy. It was just Sam Tillman takin' one of his spells."

"Was he bad?"

116

"Bad enough," the clerk told her. "But he's gone now, off in the timber. We won't see any more of him for a spell."

Amy nodded and went back upstairs. Arnie was still shaken by it all and frustrated by what appeared to be the clerks' lack of interest in the store's welfare. "Does this kind of thing go on all the time?"

"Not all the time," Loving told him, "but too often." He sighed and evened up the bolts of cloth. "When it happens . . . it just happens. There ain't no way anybody can stop a laudanum drinker, short of killin' him."

"Well," Arnie said bitterly, "I just hope we ain't got many laudanum drinkers in these parts—that's all I got to say."

"Not many," the clerk said quietly. "They don't last long."

The crowd outside the store appeared to pay very little attention to the affair. Within a matter of minutes they were back to their urgent discussions concerning weather, religion, and politics. Or, in the case of women, female complaints. Activity inside the store became hectic as the clerks worked to fill their backlog order. Arnie and Doul were back at the meat box, cutting and weighing and wrapping parcels of fat pork, when the next commotion started.

This time the disturbance was on the outside, on the side of the shed room. Well, *that's* somethin', anyhow, Arnie thought to himself. They can't wreck much out there.

Patty Doul straightened up beside Arnie, his head cocked, listening. They heard the shrieks of a few women, then a sudden ominous hush. For a moment there was no sound at all, except for the background rattling of trace chains and the stamping of the teams. A curious prickling sensation moved over the surface of Arnie's scalp.

"What is it? How come ever'body is so quiet?"

"A cuttin' scrape, most likely. Best thing's to let them settle it amongst theirselves."

"What's it about?"

"Lord knows," the young clerk said wearily. "Somebody looked cross-eyed at somebody's woman, maybe. Or a baptizin' argument between the Methodists and the Baptists. Best just stay away from it."

"What if somebody gets hisself cut open? There ain't even a doctor they can call."

"They know that."

Arnie turned toward the front of the store. Harve Purdy was unconcernedly writing in a ledger. In the back of the place Matt Loving was weighing up some rice. Arnie had the feeling that he was standing in an unnatural stillness, in the eye of a storm. He tried to go back to cutting meat, but his youthful curiosity wouldn't let him rest. With a snort of disgust, he picked up a rag and wiped his hands. "Hell's afire, we can't just stand here like nothin's happenin' and let them kill one another!"

He went out to the porch and saw two men slowly circling each other beneath the hackberry tree. A row of silent farmers stood alongside the store, watching. The women were gathered in fearful little clusters in the store yard. Nobody made a sound.

One of the fighters flashed a knife in a short, upswinging arc. The other man jumped back, but not in time. His chest and left shoulder were suddenly bright with blood. His grim, masklike expression did not change. Only his eyes changed; they were hot and there was fear in them. Arnie hurried back into the store and pulled the loaded shotgun out of the firearms case.

Purdy stared at him for a moment. "You're a fool," he said coldly, and went back to his writing.

Patty Doul grinned faintly at him and shook his head and said, "It's like I said before. Best to leave them alone."

Matt Loving looked at him with tired gray eyes but said nothing.

Arnie tucked the cheap single-barrel shotgun in the crook of his arm and returned to the porch. "That's enough," he said loudly. "If you fellers have just got to kill each other you can do it somewheres else, not here in the store yard."

The crowd turned and looked at him in amazement. Even the two fighters stopped their deadly circling and stared at him. "I mean it," Arnie told them. "Put them knives away."

A farmer in the crowd spoke up. "What do you aim to do if they don't?"

Arnie patted the shotgun. But somehow the weapon didn't look as formidable now as it had in the firearms case. Two of the younger sodbusters stepped away from the others and moved toward him. "It's a private fight. Nobody busts up a private fight."

"With a shotgun he does," Arnie said. But his voice didn't hold much conviction. More farmers stepped away from the crowd and soon there were a dozen or more hostile men cutting him off at the end of the porch. Friends or kinsmen of the combatants, Arnie guessed.

"Now go back in the store," one of them said harshly. "We'll settle this ourselves."

"Not in my store yard, you won't." As soon as Arnie heard the words he knew it was a mistake. He had closed all exits, leaving himself no way out.

One of the farmers laughed. "I don't reckon he'll be usin' that shotgun, boys. So get on back and settle your fuss the way you started."

Then Arnie made his second mistake. He raised the shotgun and fired over the heads of the fighters. They had started to back him down—he could feel himself rapidly losing control of the situation. So it had seemed a good idea to fire a shot over their heads, just to scare them and show them who was boss. It had scared them, all right. For a moment. With satisfaction Arnie watched their faces pale. Their eyes widened. But the fear was short-lived. It turned to anger. Then to rage.

A rock came out of nowhere and struck Arnie's head. It then occurred to Arnie that he was helpless. His single-barreled weapon was now useless. He fell back a step, his head ringing. A hand reached up and took the shotgun away from him. Someone else pulled him off the porch. He was sprawled on the ground, looking up at a circle of hate-filled faces.

CHAPTER SIX

The next thing Arnie knew he was stretched out on the floor of the shed room and Amy Hall was bending over him. "Lay quiet," she told him briskly, dabbing a turpentine-soaked cloth to his cut cheek.

For a few minutes he did as she ordered, trying to gather his thoughts. The last thing he remembered was falling to the ground and looking up at that ring of bitter, hostile faces. The rock flying out of nowhere. A big brogan looming in his face.

Somewhere in the distance Harve Purdy was saying with enormous satisfaction, "I told him he was a fool. Maybe next time he'll listen."

"Does that hurt?" Amy asked, dabbing his cheek with more turpentine.

Arnie winced and slowly shoved himself to a sitting position. "I'm all right now . . . I think." He made a survey of his cuts and bruises. Nothing seemed to be broken. He looked at Matt Loving, who was standing in the doorway of the shed room. "Mr. Smith," the clerk said worriedly, "there're some folks here that want to see you."

A ripple of anxiety went up Arnie's back. "You keep them crazy sodbusters away from me! I aim to have the whole bunch arrested, just as soon as I can get to Placer and find the sheriff!"

"That ain't what they're here about." Loving smiled his sad smile. "They're sorry about what happened out there—that's what they want to tell you."

Groaning, Arnie grabbed hold of a coal oil barrel and pulled himself to his feet. "Well, you can tell them all to go to hell. I've had a bait of these post oaks. I've had a bait of sodbusters."

Amy Hall was holding tightly to his arm. "It wouldn't hurt just to see them for a minute, would it, Mr. Smith?"

"I wish," Arnie told her with profound weariness, "that folks would stop callin' me Mr. Smith. Every time they do it I have to stop and look around and figger out who it is they're talkin' to."

She smiled boldly. "Will you hear what they've got to say?"

With a groan of resignation, Arnie limped into the main storeroom. Twenty or more farmers had crowded in the aisles between the counters and goods tables. Arnie regarded them with some apprehension—but their faces were not hostile or angry now. They were frightened. It was a fear in their guts that looked out of their eyes. The aura of fear hovered in the store like thunderheads on a summer day. Arnie could smell it in the air.

One of the farmers said slowly, "What we want to do, Mr. Smith, is to tell you we're sorry about what happened out there. Real sorry. Folks, they get aggravated sometimes and it looks they just got to work it out, somehow. Or fight it out. But it don't happen as a regular thing. We're askin' you to overlook it, this once. We'd be much obliged, if you did."

It's the credit, Arnie was thinking to himself. They think I'm goin' to cut off their credit—that's the thing that's got them scared cotton-mouthed and tremblin'. And for a moment he thought, By God, it would serve you right if I did it!

Then he looked at Amy Hall and saw that she was frightened too. They were all struck dumb with fear of what Arnie Smith might do. This sudden power to frighten people was one that Arnie never experienced before, and it didn't take him long to decide that he didn't like it.

Still, a man couldn't allow a bunch of sodbusters to pull him off his own porch and stomp him, and then simply shrug it off. "I ain't decided what I'm goin' to do about it," he snarled at last. "But by

God, I don't aim to have my ribs stove in as a regular thing! Ever'body better understand that!"

They stood frozen. They didn't even breathe. In anger and profound frustration, Arnie wheeled away from them, pulled down a bottle of liniment from the medicine shelf and limped back to his sleeping room. As he was rubbing some of the liniment on his battered ribs, Matt Loving appeared in the doorway.

"That was a fine thing you did in there—I just wanted to tell you that."

"We'll find out later how fine it was. Most likely it was just hammerheaded. It wouldn't surprise me if that bunch of crazy sodbusters caught me asleep some night and hacked me to pieces with a grubbin' hoe!"

Loving rocked on his heels and said nothing. "Anyhow," Arnie told him, "what would we do for customers if I started cuttin' off ever'body's credit?" He shot Loving a slitted look, but the gray clerk held his silence.

Arnie slumped to the bunk. The rage was slowly seeping out of him. "Matt," he said dejectedly, "I just don't know about these people. I don't guess I ever will."

"Maybe you ought to take that trip tomorrow. Ride out and look at the farms, talk to the people."

"And chance gettin' myself shot?"

Loving shook his head. "That's over now. A new man comin' in and takin' over the store—they were scared. A man can live with fear just so long, then . . ." He spread his hands and shrugged. "The blacksmith's got a light buggy and a tolerable bay that Mr. Syrus used to take out on a Sunday."

Arnie made a sound of resignation. "If I get shot off the seat, my blood'll be on your hands."

"Miss Amy Hall is well liked and respected. If you took her with you, nobody would start any fuss."

Suddenly Arnie felt trapped. He didn't know why.

By the time Arnie returned to the store the hitching ground was clear of wagons. Purdy was working on his books, the clerks were sorting sales tickets and replacing stock. Cautiously, Arnie climbed the stairs to the second floor. With some relief he noted that Amy had covered the table of intimate female items with a protective sheet of muslin.

"Matt Lovin' tells me you're well acquainted hereabouts."

She turned and looked at him thoughtfully. "You've got a bad lump on your head."

"It'll go down by mornin'. I aim to ride out tomorrow and look at some farms—I'd be much obliged if you'd ride along and kind of show me the way."

She nodded and showed no surprise. "I wouldn't mind. We can start right after services at Oak College."

"Do you always attend services at the school-house?"

"Of course."

"Don't you think you could skip the preachin' tomorrow, so's we could get an early start?"

"I never miss preachin'. Unless it's a case of sickness, or bad roads."

Arnie gave up. "I'll pick you up at the school-house as soon as Lovin' winds up his spiel."

As he started back down the stairs, she said with a small smile, "I'm glad everything worked out the way it did. I was afraid you wouldn't understand."

"Understand what?"

"The people here. The farmers. And how everything is so hard for them now."

"Ma'am," Arnie told her with a good deal of feeling, "I'll tell you the honest truth. I don't understand a thing in the world about these sodbusters. And that's a fact."

The blacksmith's "tolerable bay" was a hard-mouthed mare of advanced age and sour disposition. The "light buggy" was a conglomeration of many vehicles that the smith had salvaged one place and another and patched together with *bois d'arc* splints and scraps of iron. It was an ungainly and awkward rig, but it was stout and substantial, as any rig had to be in order to navigate the deep-rutted country roads.

Arnie turned onto the Oak College hitching

ground just as Loving's congregation was winding up a rousing chorus of "Beulah Land." There were ten wagons and several saddle animals tied up in front of the building, but the meeting itself was in the "summer church," a dozen or so homemade benches beneath a sheltering brush arbor, in back of the schoolhouse. This is where regular church and protracted meetings were held. Where politicians held their rallies, where traveling minstrels performed. A place for parties and country dances, and funerals, and weddings. It was, almost as an afterthought, a place where children of the area were educated. For a year or so. Providing they could be spared from the fields and their everyday chores at home. Providing they had reasonably decent clothes to wear, and if the parents didn't look upon all schooling as so much frivolity. This was where Amy Hall performed her duties as a teacher.

Arnie smoked a cigarette while Matt Loving wandered through a long and rambling prayer in which the Lord was asked to change the weather, cure a variety of blights, and raise the price of cotton. The meeting began to break up. Farmers in their shapeless jean suits, the women in gingham dresses, gathered in clusters for what would be their last chance to gossip for another week. Some of them broke out lunches of cold biscuits and fried meat and spring onions. The ones who noticed Arnie at all glanced at him with quick and fearful eyes and then quickly looked away.

At last Amy Hall broke away from a group that was busily shaking hands with Matt Loving. On weekdays Loving was just another clerk in a country store; on Sundays he was a man of some importance. Amy headed toward the blacksmith's buggy carrying a small parcel wrapped in brown paper.

"Most likely we'll be out the rest of the day," she said. "I brought a lunch to last us till suppertime."

Arnie was embarrassed, for he had already learned that, in the post oaks, food was not a thing to be given away on a whim. "I never thought about havin' to eat. I could of brought somethin' from the store."

She smiled. "I was hopin' you'd be here in time to hear the message."

"I get to hear Matt every day at the store."

"He spoke about charity. 'Charity suffereth long and is kind; charity envieth not: charity vaunteth not itself, is not puffed up.' That's from First Corinthians."

"Charity starts at home is the way I always heard it."

Amy laughed as Arnie helped her up to the black leather seat. As they pulled away from the schoolhouse, Arnie asked, "Did Matt say anything in that message about pullin' your neighbor down off the porch and kickin' him when he's down?"

". . . I think that's what he was talkin' about. Most men would have wanted to hit back. What you did was a charitable thing. That's what he wanted them to understand."

"It ain't that I didn't *want* to hit back. They never gave me the chance."

"I don't mean that. You could have hurt them much worse than they hurt you, simply by stopping their credit."

"That," Arnie said defensively, "would of been poor business. Even I know that much."

She looked at him curiously. "I didn't realize you were such a dedicated businessman."

"All I want is to get this store off my hands. And it stands to reason that there ain't nobody goin' to buy a store that's doin' a poor business."

". . . I see." They rode for the next several minutes in silence. After a while she pointed toward a patch of sickly young cotton. "That's our place. The Hall place. One reason I took the teachin' job is because it's an easy walk to the schoolhouse." Her smile was a trifle uneasy. "We're on the books at Smith's store, like everybody else. You might as well start your lookin' here."

Before leaving the store Arnie had made a list of places that he wanted to look at. He had copied down a few facts about each place that Harve Purdy had considered important—the number of acres, how many acres were planted to corn, how many to cotton. What kind of shape the house and barns were in, the number and kind of livestock. He hadn't made a list on the Hall place because he hadn't intended to look at it today. But since he was here—he shrugged—why not?

They turned off the almost impassable road onto a worse one. What Arnie saw he found depressing. The young cotton plants grew thickly in long rows, but they looked limp and lifeless, much less vigorous than the green grass that was growing up around the slender stalks. Arnie had had very little experience at cotton farming, but he knew that the plants had to be thinned and kept clear of grass. In the distance he could see the house and barn and two small sheds, all of them gray and unpainted. They seemed to be sinking slowly into the ground.

Arnie said, "Has your pa put in any corn?"

Amy shook her head. "Most folks put in some, a little, but Mr. Syrus and Harve Purdy never did like it. It's easier to keep check on a place if there's just one crop to keep track of."

Arnie had wondered, vaguely, why the farmers planted cotton and very little else. Now he knew. It made Purdy's bookkeeping easier.

Most likely that was the reason they ran out of home-cured meat before the year was half over and had to buy the dry salt pork from the store. The saying was that farmers liked pork but hated hogs—but maybe they had simply been afraid of riling Syrus Smith and Harve Purdy.

Still, this had nothing to do with the sorry, unworked patch of cotton that Arnie was looking at. The more he saw, the more embarrassed both of them became. When they came to a wide place in the road, Arnie turned the buggy around. "I'll look at your pa's place some other time, after I look it up in the books."

Amy smiled faintly. "My pa ain't much of a farmer. I have to admit that much."

"How does he make a go of it?"

She shrugged. "We've got a cow and a few chickens. Butter and eggs help. Pecans and walnuts in the fall. And my teachin' at Oak College."

They jolted along on the uneven road, and from time to time Arnie would squirm in his ill-fitting shirt. Suddenly he asked, "Can you sew?"

The question surprised her. "How do you mean?"

"Can you make things? Shirts, pants, things like that."

"If I had a machine."

"There's one at the store. Figger it up sometime. The amount of hickory it would take to make a shirt—a shirt that don't cut off a man's circulation every time he stoops over. Buttons, thread, things like that. If you can make a shirt for less than the ones we've got at the store, why we'll sell them at the same price and the difference will be your profit."

For a moment he saw excitement in her eyes— but it quickly faded. She shook her head. "Harve Purdy never would allow the Halls enough credit to buy a machine with."

"Do your figgerin' anyhow. I'll talk to Purdy."

The first name on Arnie's list was Fred Medder. Medder's crops appeared to be reasonably well along, considering the dry spring. The animals were in fair shape, repairs had been kept up on the barn.

The house was another story. Delly Medder met them at the door, smiling blankly. She invited Arnie and Amy Hall into the shambles of a kitchen. "Set down, make yourself to home. I'll make you some herb tea."

But she forgot to make the tea. From the looks of the house, she had forgotten a lot of things. The stove was cold, dirty dishes were piled in a granite pan, a heavy layer of dust and grease lay on everything. Arnie recalled the Medders were carried on the books for a medium bottle of morphine every week. He left the house feeling depressed but told Fred Medder, "That cotton ought to come along fine, if we get some rain."

Two small children clung to the farmer's legs. Their eyes seemed abnormally large; their skin looked sweaty and seemed to be pulled tightly over the bones of their faces. Arnie noticed that they moved slowly and with apparent difficulty, like old men. They looked half dead of starvation, although Arnie knew there was food in the house and that Fred Medder was not the type of man to let children go hungry.

When they were on the road again, Arnie asked,

"How long has Mrs. Medder been at the morphine?"

"About two years. Since she lost her last baby with the summer complaint."

There didn't seem to be anything more to say on that subject. He added up Fred Medder's potential in his mind and decided that it wouldn't be practical to increase his monthly rate of credit. On the other hand, he wouldn't cut it.

They stopped along the road for a lunch of cold biscuits and fried chicken and mashed potato salad. Arnie realized that this was a feast, in the post oaks, and it was in his honor—although he didn't quite understand why. "There was a time," he said, picking the last bone clean, "when I figgered I could live out my life on cove oysters and sardines and not ever ask for anything better. I'm startin' to learn that store grub can be as common as trail grub, if you get enough of it."

She smiled, then for no apparent reason said, "Fred Medder is a good man, and a good farmer too." She wanted to ask if Arnie meant to cut the Medder credit, but she didn't. She saw a certain look in Arnie's eyes, almost of pain, and she asked quickly, "Is anything wrong?"

Arnie shook his head. "I don't know. Back when I was workin' cows . . ." *Had that been only two weeks ago? It didn't seem possible.* "When I was workin' cows, I knowed a lot of trail bosses and straw bosses of one kind or another. Big men, they was. Rich and powerful. All the same, I never seen a cow boss so powerful that a common cowhand was scared of him. Here it's different. I look a sod-buster in the eye and I can see his gizzard curl up and try to hide behind his liver. I never had folks to be scared of me before. I don't like it."

"It's not you, it's the store."

"The store ain't Godamighty."

"It is almost, to some of them. The ones with babies that are hungry or need medicine. The ones with wives like Delly Medder."

Well, Arnie thought glumly, there's another subject that's come to a dead end. He fell into a moody silence, and after a while he saw Amy looking at him in a strange way. "Ever since that ruckus at the store," he told her, "I've been thinkin' about that laudanum drinker. What's his name?"

"Sam Tillman."

"That's the one. I've knowed about laudanum drinkers for a long time, of course. There's plenty of them, all over. But Tillman's the only one I ever seen right up close. Is there many more like him in these parts?"

She shook her head sadly. "Thank the Lord, no. Up till about a year ago Mr. Tillman was packer at the cotton gin at Placer. Then there was an accident—somethin' to do with the presses—and Doc McPhitter kept him dosed up with laudanum, on account of the pain. Well, when Mr. Tillman got better he had this cravin' for laudanum that he says is even worse than the pain. Ever since then he's been . . . well, you saw."

Arnie had heard about some doctors who, when they didn't know what else to do, which was most of the time, kept their patients dosed up on opium or morphine or laudanum. Landanum was the worst. "Maybe," Arnie said slowly, "I ought to take all that dope off the shelves and not stock it any more."

"Maybe," she said, but without real conviction. There would still be doctors like McPhitter. And "friends" like Sam Tillman, who had once been a quiet and gentle man, they said. And women like Delly Medder. It was a subject of which she had thought about a good deal over the years, but she didn't know the answer.

By the end of the afternoon Arnie had inspected four farms and glimpsed half a dozen others. What he had seen did not fill him with confidence in the country or its people. With too many of the farmers the mask of defeat had settled on their faces. Cotton was going unchopped. Grass was growing up between the rows. If the grass don't kill it, the general opinion seemed to be, the dry weather will. Or the insects. Or the rot.

The last name on the list of farms to be inspected was that of Croy Mackerson. "Croy," said Arnie wearily, eying the rows of stunted plants, "that crop ain't never goin' to amount to a damn unless you keep it chopped."

Mackerson nodded in sorrowful agreement. "I know. Ever' mornin' I go out with a hoe, but by dinnertime I'm played out. Me and Mr. King too. That's my wife's pa; he lives here and helps with the work."

"What's the matter? Are you sick?"

Croy Mackerson thought about this for a moment. "I'm poorly in my spirit, I guess," he said at last. "Ever' mornin' I go out with the hoe, like I said. By dinnertime it just don't seem like it's worth the bother. I know it's wrong, and I give myself a good talkin' to. But I don't know . . ." His voice trailed off. "It's the hard times, I guess."

The farmer's depression was so profound that Arnie didn't have the heart to upbraid him. Then, quite suddenly, the farmer's eyes turned bright with panic. "You ain't goin' to shut off my credit, are you, Mr. Smith? I promise to clear out that grass. Next time you're out this way I'll have the purtiest cotton patch in the post oaks. You'll see."

"All right, Croy," Arnie said helplessly. "I don't aim to shut off your credit. Don't fret about it." He started to walk away, then thought of something and came back. "Croy, have you put in a garden for vegetables yet?"

The farmer turned strangely defensive. "Well, I guess I did plow up a little patch, and Flower, my wife, put out a few onion sets, and a few hills of potatoes. It ain't much."

"Is that all? Why didn't you plant greens, turnips, okra, stuff like that?"

Croy eyed him suspiciously. "Why, Mr. Syrus never was much of a hand for gardens. Ain't no money in gardens, that's what Mr. Syrus said. Spend your time in the fields. Cotton, that's what you got to raise, if you aim to settle your bill at the store at the end of the year."

Arnie made a sound of exasperation. "Next time you're in the store pick up some seed—it still ain't too late to plant. Might be you won't feel so 'poorly in your spirit' with a bait of collard greens in your belly."

A cluster of stairstep children huddled near the back door of the house. Arnie noted the same too-large eyes and sweaty skin and knobby limbs that he had been noticing all day. Turning the buggy back toward the store, he barked angrily to Amy Hall, "What kind of folks have you got here? Ain't they got no sense at all? Even an ignorant cowhand knows that a body can't do a good day's work on a steady feed of sowbelly and corn bread."

Amy stiffened beside him. "Farmers know it too." Then, in a gentler tone, "Did you mean it, what you said about allowing them to plant gardens?"

"Of course I mean it," Arnie said indignantly. "Any fool can see that the whole bunch is about to come down with the summer complaint if they don't change their feed. *Then* where would the

137

store be? I don't know why it took me the whole day to figger it out."

Amy was curiously silent for a long while. Then, as the buggy turned onto the red clay road to her father's place, she said quietly, "It was a good thing for all of us, the sodbusters, when you took charge of the store, Arnie Smith."

"Sure," Arnie said bitterly. "That's why they hauled me off the porch and stomped me."

"They didn't know you then. They were afraid, and folks do crazy things when they're afraid."

It seemed to Arnie that he had covered this ground before. "Much obliged," he said, "for the grub and for ridin' out with me today." He helped her down from the buggy and then drove back to the store.

It was dark by the time he got back, and there was a lamp burning in the tiny post office cubicle where Harve Purdy did his bookwork. "Well," the bookkeeper said as Arnie came in the front door, "you've been out long enough, seems like. Did you and Miss Amy look at any farms while you was gone?"

Purdy's implication was that they hadn't been looking at farms at all—and Arnie didn't like it. He slammed the door, bolted it on the inside and immediately began going through the small display of garden seed.

"Purdy, is this all the seed we've got in the store?"

The bookkeeper grunted. "Don't get much call for garden seed hereabouts."

"How long will it take to get some more?"

"Six weeks if you're lucky. Six months if you ain't." Purdy pushed his spectacles down on his nose and squinted. "Anyhow, we don't need them. I already told you there ain't much call."

"I figger things are about to change. Write up an order for beans, squash, okra, turnips, stuff like that. Get it off on the next stage."

"It wouldn't get here in time to do any good, even if there was somebody that wanted to plant a garden. Which there ain't."

Arnie turned and looked at Purdy through the grilled window. "Purdy," he said with failing patience, "there's one thing that you've got trouble gettin' straight in your head. You're the hand and I'm the boss. I don't know how you're used to doin' it here, but in cow country the boss gives the orders and the hand carries them out. Or he quits."

Prudy's face turned pale in the flickering lamplight. "Are you tellin' me to draw my time?"

"I'm tellin' you there can't be but one boss, and I'm him." In some closed part of his mind Arnie realized that he was digging himself in deeper and deeper, and what he was digging was probably his own grave. But, like Croy Mackerson, he was feeling poorly in his spirit. He had seen too many faces stamped with defeat that day. Too many undernourished bodies. And the memory of Delly

Medder and the laudanum drinker still haunted him. Well, he thought to himself, there was nothing he could do about Mrs. Medder and Sam Tillman, but there might be something he could do for the children.

In the back of his mind, ever since his talk with Mackerson, a highly impractical and probably dangerous thought had been growing. Maybe Croy had said about everything there was to say about hard times on the farm. He had seen too many crops die in the ground. His hope had quietly eroded, like the dry, black earth in which he dug. After a while it didn't seem worth while to go on working. Arnie could understand that. What did he have to work for? Twenty-five dollars a month in credit at the Smith General Mercantile Company? Less credit charges and interest. A few pounds of fat pork and a small sack of corn meal? Maybe it wasn't much wonder that Croy was feeling poorly in spirit.

That dangerous thought in the back of Arnie's mind kept on growing. He looked at Purdy for a long time, and finally he said, "One of the farms I looked at today was Croy Mackerson's place."

Lamplight glinted on the bookkeeper's spectacles. "Well, now you know what kind of farmer he is. I told you yesterday he wasn't worth half the twenty-five dollars he's bein' carried for on the books."

Arnie said, "I've decided to stretch his credit to thirty. Maybe that's what he needs to get him goin' again. A quart of molasses to take home with him on a Saturday. A piece of bolt goods for his woman."

Purdy couldn't have been more shocked if Arnie had suddenly drawn a gun and shot him. "You're out of your head! The store'll go bust if you start givin' more credit!"

"To tell you the truth," Arnie said wearily, "I don't much give a damn."

Arnie turned to go to his sleeping room. White-faced, Purdy hollered, "Smith!" He couldn't bring himself to call the owner "Mr. Smith," and neither could he call him "Arnie." "Smith," he said again in bitter anger. "I tell you you're drivin' the store to bankruptcy!"

"If she goes bust she goes bust."

"I won't be responsible! I'll quit first!"

There it was. Only Purdy understood all the mysteries of the Smith General Mercantile Company. It was all written down in the heavy leatherbound books in the post office cubicle, like the hieroglyphics of an ancient secret order. Now Purdy was threatening to quit. This was his ultimate weapon. He would simply roll down his sleeves and walk out. Let the ignorant cowhand struggle a while with double-entry bookkeeping—he'd come around soon enough.

Arnie could read it all in Purdy's tightly pursed mouth and bullet eyes. But a strange mood was upon him. He refused to allow Purdy's threat to stampede him. "If that's the way you feel," he said, "draw your time."

He walked through the dark store to the musty-smelling box that was his sleeping room. "Now that was a fool thing for me to do," he said aloud, as he lit the coal oil lamp. "The store won't last a week without somebody to read the books and tell me where I'm goin'." He sat for a long while, staring at the plank walls. A spider was busily spinning an intricate web in a corner above the doorway. The yellow store cat was asleep on the bunk. Arnie scratched the cat's ears and the animal stretched and yawned widely and went back to sleep. "Some mouser. Like ever'thing else in the post oaks—not worth a damn for anything."

What I ought to do, he thought, is hurry back in there before Purdy gets away and beg his pardon and try to get him to stay. But he didn't do it. After a while he heard the bookkeeper slamming angrily through the double front doors. Then he circled around to the blacksmith shed where he stabled his mule, and Arnie heard the animal plodding off to the west through the thickets to the small farm where Purdy lived with his brother's family.

Arnie went back in the store and bolted the front doors from the inside, then locked the back door as he came out. He looked in amazement at the moon rising over the scrub timber. "What the hell am I doin' here? Why don't I just pack up and leave? Who wants a damn country store anyhow?"

142

Pack what? The store was all he had.

He returned to his sleeping room and rummaged until he located a ruled writing tablet and a pencil. The spider was still spinning. The yellow cat purred contentedly.

Dear Lawyer Webber. I sure do hope you've located a buyer for this store because if you ain't I'm a blowed up sucker . . .

CHAPTER SEVEN

The next morning after Arnie had filled his lungs with clean fresh air and boiled a pot of Arbuckle's coffee on the monkey stove, the world did not look like such an unpleasant place after all. It was easy to convince himself—youth being the thing it was—that Purdy would settle himself behind the grilled window as always and everything would be as it was before.

But Purdy did not come. Matt Loving arrived on foot at daybreak, carrying his small lunch parcel. "Hasn't Harve got here yet?"

"I told him to draw his time last night."

The gray clerk looked stunned.

"Why would you do a thing like that?"

As briefly as possible Arnie explained about the vegetable seed and the credit. Loving's gray head went up and down in sympathy, but when Arnie finished he said, "I'm afraid it was a mistake gettin' Harve riled. He's the only bookkeeper in these parts. And he knowed the store as well as Mr. Syrus hisself. You figger he just aims to give you a scare and then come back?"

"I figger bookkeepin' jobs is as scarce as book-keepers. If he wants to work hereabouts, here's the place he's got to come to."

Loving shook his head sadly. "I don't know. Harve's got a powerful stubborn streak in him."

By the end of the week Arnie began to appreciate how stubborn. "Keep track of all the sales tickets and written orders," he told the clerk. "That's about all we can do until we get some help."

He wrote another desperate letter to Lawyer Webber. The lawyer replied that he had rounded up several prospects, but considering the tight money and hard times in general, a sale was apt to take considerable time.

Time was something Arnie didn't have. With every business transaction—with every bottle of snuff or pound of corn meal that went out of the store—the records were thrown into more desperate confusion. Arnie and Matt Loving watched another Saturday approach as they would have watched the approach of Armageddon. On Friday afternoon Arnie did something that he vowed he would never do.

He borrowed the blacksmith's bay and rode out to the small farm where Purdy lived with his brother's family. It was a poor piece of ground, full of rocks and grass, with post oak seedlings slowly drawing a strangling belt around the edges. The house and sheds were unpainted and weathered gray. There was an unmistakable aura of poverty about the place—and out of this air of misery Arnie drew some hope.

In these times of harsh depression it didn't stand to reason that a man would refuse a cash-paying job, even if it meant working for somebody you hated. Arnie dismounted in the dooryard and helloed. A dog barked in the distance. A few chickens clucked and scratched in the gravelly earth. In a nearby field there were two men, a woman, and several children chopping cotton. One of the men was Harve Purdy.

Arnie helloed again, and one of the men slowly shouldered his hoe and plodded toward the house. It wasn't Harve, it was an older, tireder, faded copy of the bookkeeper. "Mr. Purdy?" Arnie asked.

The farmer nodded wearily. "That's right, Whit Purdy. And you're Mr. Syrus's nephew from the store, I guess."

"Yes, sir. I guess you know about . . ."

"I know all about it. Heard it often enough this past week. Harve said you'd come beggin' him to take his job back."

Something cold settled in the pit of Arnie's stomach. "Well, I never come out here to beg, exactly." Although both of them knew better. "But I did come to offer Harve his job back."

"Harve said tell you he ain't interested. He ain't

145

comin' back." Whit Purdy cleared his throat and went on in a quieter voice. "Maybe he means it. It's hard to tell about Harve. I'm his brother, but I'd be the first to tell you that."

"You mean there's a chance he *will* come back?"

"I mean it don't make sense, the way he's doin'. He says he can't go back on account of his pride. But pride don't fill a man's belly or save his farm."

"You figger it would do any good if I went and asked him?"

"It wouldn't hurt to try."

Purdy was inexpertly hacking at the grass and thinning the stalks of cotton. He did not look up as Arnie approached. "Harve," Arnie said with determined good humor, "you got the best of me. You was right from the first—it sure looks like the store'll go bust if you don't take over the books."

Harve paused and rested on his hoe. "I told them you'd come beggin'."

Arnie swallowed with great difficulty. "Well, it looks like you was right. I'm here. I'm askin' you to come back."

The bookkeeper looked at him sourly. "I don't think so."

Arnie exploded. "God damn it, can't you see how hammerheaded you're bein'! If the store goes bust, ever'body goes bust. You and your brother, as well as ever'body else."

Purdy smiled grimly. "If I *was* to come back—

which ain't sayin' I will—there's got to be some changes made."

"Changes?" Again Arnie felt that coldness in his stomach. "What kind of changes?"

"Cut back on the credit, like I told you in the first place. And stop that foolishness about vegetable gardens. Mr. Syrus never allowed any of that."

There they were at the end of the road, with an insurmountable wall of hostility standing between them. Arnie heard himself hollering, "Purdy, you're a hammerheaded fool! It's my store and I aim to run it the way that suits me!"

The bookkeeper pulled himself up with dignity. "Before the month's out the banks will have you."

"Is that all you want, just to see me fail?"

Purdy clamped his jaw and went back to chopping cotton. He did not look up again.

"It's no good," Arnie told Matt Loving when he returned to the store. "Purdy figgers he's got me over a barrel. He figgers he can make me crawl and beg, just because my uncle left him out of his will. Well, to hell with him. I'll see the place go bust first!"

The gray clerk had that faraway look that he usually reserved for Sunday preaching. "Lord help this poor land, and its people."

"Lord help Arnie Smith," Arnie said bitterly. "He ain't even got a decent pair of boots. All he's got is a bankrupt country store." Then he took a deep breath and let it out with a whistle. "Well, tomorrow I'll catch the stage to Placer and talk to that lawyer. Maybe he can think of somethin'."

"Tomorrow's Saturday."

Appalled, Arnie stared at the clerk with his mouth open. Saturday or Doomsday—without a bookkeeper, it was all the same.

Actually, Saturday passed with only one cutting scrape and two minor injuries. A day of unusual tranquillity, considering that it was a typical country store in Texas, on a Saturday afternoon. In the upstairs section of the store the farm wives waited on themselves while Amy Hall improvised a filing system of pasteboard boxes in an attempt to keep track of what had been sold, and for how much, and to whom. Arnie worked at the meat box, where the main requirement was the stamina of youth and a strong back, and Loving and Patty Doul filled orders in the front part of the store.

When the day was finally over Arnie straightened his aching back, washed his hands and arms, and limped up front to the post office window. Amy Hall smiled wanly and shook her head. "I think I've got all the tickets sorted, but I can't make heads or tails out of Harve's bookkeepin'."

Arnie nodded dejectedly. "Abe Cutter left his horse and his rig," he said, "in case I wanted to look at farms tomorrow. I'll ride you home as soon as I get the stock covered."

It was a cool, star-studded night with a taste of

dust and summer in the air. For some time they jolted over the rough road in silence. Then Arnie said wistfully, "When I was a cowhand I used to cuss the way I had to live. Long hours in the saddle. Sleepin' in the rain. Livin' in dread that your horse would go off a cut bank some dark night. Or stumble in front of a stampede. Or a bolt of lightnin' would knock you out of the saddle." He turned to Amy and grinned. "I never thought I'd look back on them days and think they was easy."

"Is keepin' store so hard?"

"Not for a storekeeper, maybe." He turned the blacksmith's buggy into the Hall dooryard.

"Much obliged for helpin' out today."

She made an agreeable sound. "I've been thinkin' about that machine. Now that Harve's not at the store any more, do you think the Hall credit could be stretched enough to buy it?"

She said it as a joke, but Arnie understood that she wasn't joking. He said, "I'll get Abe Cutter to load that sewin' machine and haul it over to you first thing Monday mornin'." It was easy to be a big man when you owned the only store in a place like Smith, Texas. You simply threw your head back importantly and promised whatever folks wanted to hear. Of course, in the meantime the store was falling down around his shoulders—but best not to think too much about that.

When he got back, the store was dark. Loving and Doul had covered the goods tables with muslin dust sheets. They looked like giant corpses laid out for some heroic funeral. "What I need," Arnie groaned to himself, "is some sleep and rest. I feel like I been swimmin' a thousand head of cattle across a risin' river all day."

But he was too nervous to sleep. He lit a coal oil lamp and wandered about. Idly, he counted items on the shelves, making mental reminders of stock that needed to be replaced. After a while he realized what he was doing and pulled up in amazement. He had known cowmen who could not rest out of sight of their own herds. They built their houses on top of hills so that they could always look out and see their cattle. Arnie wondered, "Am I gettin' to be the same way about this damn store?"

With a snort of disgust, he blew out the lamp and headed for his sleeping room. Tomorrow he would go to Placer and talk to the lawyer, and between the two of them maybe they could figure out a way to get the place off his hands.

But the next day he didn't go to Placer.

The next day the scavengers came.

In time of war the scavengers always came. In time of disaster and panic and misery. They were an inseparable part of what was generally thought of as "hard times," but a part that Arnie had never encountered before.

They arrived at Smith, Texas, at about five o'clock that Sunday morning.

First there was a gunshot. Arnie sat bolt upright in alarm. Quickly, he got out of his bunk and pulled on his pants. Barefooted and blind he blundered about the sleeping room looking for a gun. But Arnie Smith, the storekeeper, no longer wore a gun. Even though he owned more than a dozen, they were in the firearms case in the store. He fumbled for some other kind of weapon, but the only thing he could find was the heavy glass base of a lamp. That would have to do.

He raised the latch and eased the door open. In the iron-hard light of first dawn he saw the horses hitched in the open space between the back of the store and the blacksmith shed. He counted up to a dozen and stopped. Inside the store he heard the sound of voices, the muffled curses and laughter as men blundered about in the darkness. Someone upset a goods table and Arnie heard the heavy bolts of cloth thudding to the floor like dead bodies.

In a rage he took a firm hold on the lamp base and stepped out to the loading platform that ran alongside the sleeping room. He saw the useless lock to the back door hanging on its chain, blasted apart by a single well-placed bullet. "Well," Arnie thought grimly, "now I know what the shootin' was about."

A streak of yellow light appeared suddenly beneath the door. Someone had found a lamp and lit it. Arnie stood for a moment, his thoughts milling angrily. Who were these men? What were they doing here? How was he going to deal with them?

It was then that the scavenger lookout came quietly up behind him, aimed carefully at the back of his head, and swung with the stock of his rifle.

A flash of light burst inside Arnie's head. I've been shot! was his first thought. After years of ridin' with armed cowhands, I have to come to a country store to get myself shot!

He fell to his knees and dropped his lamp. He heard the shattering glass and smelled the coal oil. Everything was very clear and distinct for a moment. He threw out his arms to break his fall, but his arms gave way and he fell with his face on the rough planking of the platform.

When he came to he was looking up at a circle of faces. "It's gettin' to be a habit," he thought through a roaring pain in his head. Once before he had regained consciousness this way, looking up at a circle of hostile sodbuster faces.

But these men were not sodbusters. They had grayish dull faces, like lumps of putty. In some strange way they all looked alike, and Arnie slowly realized that it was because they were all wearing masks of dirt and grime, the accumulation of weeks or months of a very special kind of filth. The filth that a man accumulates when he is on the run and has neither the time nor the inclination to wash.

Fourteen pairs of sharp, wolflike eyes looked

down at him. Fourteen jaws worked rhythmically as they stuffed their mouths with cheese and pickles and salmon and sardines and crackers. Fourteen Adam's apples went up and down as they gulped the store's best Maryland Bourbon from tin cups, also the store's. Some of them grinned loosely when they saw that Arnie was beginning to come to life. Some of them scowled. Most of them only stared blankly.

One of the scavengers nudged Arnie with the toe of his brogan. "Come alive, boy. I want to talk to you."

Arnie started to sit up. The floor of the store tilted sickeningly and he fell over on his face. One of the scavengers laughed. The first man, the one who seemed to be the leader of the bunch, nudged Arnie again with his foot, a little harder this time. "You got a right smart knock on the head, boy, but you'll live. If you behave." He hunkered down so that his face was on a level with Arnie's. In one filthy hand he clutched a fistful of smacks, in the other a pickle. He ate some of the ginger snaps, then took a bite of pickle. He grinned. "Where you keep the money, boy?"

Obviously the scavenger knew even less than Arnie about country stores. One thing a store like Smith's almost never had on hand was cash money. Plenty of notes and liens and mortgages, and some-times bank drafts from the cotton gins in the fall. But almost never cash. Even the rare remnants of cattle outfits that passed this way, between Louisiana and the Indian Territory, never left cash for the supplies they bought. The brand on their wagon or on their company horses was as good as the recommendation of the biggest bank in Texas; they took what they needed and paid when they got around to it.

"Mister," Arnie heard himself saying in a voice that was thin and sickly, "there ain't any cash money in this store. You can tear it apart and burn it down, and you won't find more'n a dollar or two, and that's over there behind the post office window."

The leader said, "Bonny, see what you can find."

A young man, still in his teens, flung away a piece of cheese and slouched to the post office window. He lit another lamp and rummaged for several minutes. "Two silver dollars and a two-bit piece," he announced disgustedly when he returned.

"That's government money," Arnie said recklessly. "You better put it back without you want a passel of United States deputies on your tail."

The man who seemed to be the leader found this amusing. He chuckled. "I like you, boy. You got spunk." He rocked back on his heels and filled his mouth with smacks. "You ever hear of Frank Carr, boy?"

Arnie shook his head and was instantly sorry. There was so much pain in his head that his eyes

154

seemed to bulge. His mouth was as dry as cotton; he would have given a great deal for a drink of water. "No, I don't recollect ever hearin' about anybody by the name of Frank Carr."

"You will," the scavenger said confidently, taking a bite of pickle.

"Are you Frank Carr?"

"That's right. We just come down from the Choctaw Nation, so don't tell us about United States deputies. We been makin' fools out of the United States deputies for nigh as long as I can remember. Ain't that right, Bonny?"

The young scavenger grunted indifferently. "Maybe he's tellin' the truth, Frank. Maybe there ain't any money. Why don't we just take what we want and light out before trouble comes."

"That's the trouble with bein' young and full of vinegar," Frank Carr said to Arnie. "No patience. If you *was* to have some money hereabouts, you wouldn't tell us about it, first crack out of the barrel, would you? Young'uns don't stop to think about things like that."

"You already found all the money there is. There ain't any more."

"Bonny," Frank Carr said, "you take some of the boys upstairs and have a look-see."

"Daylight's comin' on. I don't figger we ought to be hangin' around much longer."

"Nobody told you to figger. Do like I say."

The young scavenger and half a dozen others

155

climbed the stairs. Arnie winced as he heard the place being systematically wrecked. Frank Carr opened a can of sardines and ate them leisurely. "You know what the settlers call folks like us, boy? Scavengers. We don't mind. The thing to remember is that we get what we come after—or, if we don't, we don't leave nothin' for anybody else. Now are you startin' to see how it's goin' to be?"

Arnie's head throbbed. He looked around at all those putty faces. "What I see is you're goin' to get yourself in a mess of trouble. This ain't the Choctaw Nation you're in, it's Texas. We got law."

Frank Carr chuckled contentedly. "Because you're green and ignorant I'll tell you how we do things, boy. Then if somethin' bad happens, you got nobody to blame but yourself." He paused, listening to the noise upstairs. "First off," he continued, "we ask you, nice and polite. Like we already done. Then we wreck a little bit of your place. We start upstairs and break whatever we can find. Then we ask you again, nice and polite. If you don't tell us what we want to know, we start at the back of the store and work to the front, and we smash and break everything in between. If that still don't satisfy you, we set fire to the place and burn it down. Then . . ." The dirty mask smiled. "Then we kill you."

Arnie sighed hopelessly. There was not the slightest doubt in his mind that Frank Carr would do everything he promised. Very carefully, he took hold of a counter top and pulled himself to his feet. "I still don't have any money," he said. "You can tear the place down, and burn it, and then kill me, but there still ain't any money."

The scavenger shrugged. He didn't seem particularly angry; it was just that he had started something and meant to see it through to the end. He turned toward the stairway and hollered, "Bonny, get yourself down here. We got work to do."

Bonny and his fellow scavengers tramped back down the stairs. Frank Carr took a seat on the thread counter and lit one of the store's best rum-cured cigars. "Look around," he said, waving the cigar magnanimously. "Take what you want for yourself, then we'll start at the back and wreck the place proper."

Arnie stared with the look of a man who had come awake to find that his nightmare was real. The scavengers strolled through the store, upsetting tables and counters, stripping shelves, casually stuffing their pockets with dollar watches, pistols, small bottles of perfume, tobacco and cigars. Within five minutes the Smith General Mercantile Company looked like one giant trash heap—and they hadn't even started their serious wrecking yet.

Frank Carr grinned at Arnie. "I don't reckon you've changed your mind about tellin' us where the money is?"

Arnie felt a crazy wildness taking hold of him. Is this what Syrus Smith had worked a lifetime for, just to have a bunch of stinking scavengers pull it down and burn it? "There ain't no money!" His voice had gone suddenly shrill.

Carr grinned indifferently and motioned his wrecking crew back to the rear of the store. "We may be scavengers, boys, but it's time we showed the greenhorn that when we start a job we finish it in first-class order."

One of the putty faces laughed. Someone found a crowbar and began to rip a medicine shelf off the wall. Arnie stared in dismay as the bottles crashed to the floor. Tables were turned over. Heavy bolts of cloth were unwound and torn and trampled on. They were very businesslike—when an item was overlooked or undestroyed, Frank Carr would call one of the men back to attend to it.

The line of scavengers moved through the store like a plague of locusts through a cornfield. They smashed and ripped and broke with machinelike efficiency.

Carr looked at Arnie and shook his head sorrowfully. "Maybe there really ain't any money. Too bad."

Arnie's eyes bulged in helpless rage. "Make them stop! What good'll it do you, bustin' up the place like this?"

The scavenger flipped his cigar away and casually lit another. "The next place we go to, maybe they'll of heard about what happened here. And they won't be in no big hurry to be stubborn."

"I ain't bein' stubborn!" Arnie yelled in frustration. "There ain't any money!"

"Tell you the honest truth," Frank Carr sighed, "I believe you, boy. It don't stand to reason that a body would stand by and see his store wrecked on account of a few measly dollars he might have put away somewheres. But when you're a scavenger you got to behave like a scavenger—that's what makes folks scared of you. You can understand that, can't you?"

Arnie could understand that all the pain and indignities that he had endured these past two weeks had been for nothing. Being waylaid by the sodbusters, losing the only decent clothes he had, and finally being stomped by more sodbusters in his own store yard. But this plague of scavengers was the crowning indignity of all.

The fancy goods case—a glass case of cheap trinkets—crashed to the floor. Something inside Arnie seemed to snap. He watched the amber combs and stickpins and glass-set brooches being ground beneath the feet of the scavengers, and a wildness rushed through him.

He heard himself screaming. Frank Carr thought it was funny; he rocked back on the thread counter and laughed until his eyes watered. This only made Arnie wilder. He threw himself at one of the wreckers and received a savage blow alongside the head for his trouble. He lunged again and got a heavy brogan in his chest. Frank Carr rolled on the thread counter, holding his sides. He was making choking sounds, laughing until he could hardly get his breath.

Then, with the suddenness of shattering glass, the scavenger was laughing no longer. He stared at Arnie, his eyes bulging. The advancing line of scavengers also stopped and stared. As if by magic, Arnie was suddenly holding a shotgun in his hands.

"Don't do nothin' crazy, boys," Frank Carr said at last. "It's his play party now. Just let him be."

But the young scavenger known as Bonny was in no mood to let it be. He sneered at Arnie and grabbed for his pistol.

One part of Arnie's mind was racing wildly, out of control; another part was eerily cool and rational. The loaded shotgun had come from the firearms case where it was normally kept. He had simply picked it up off the floor—with so much litter and wreckage, no one had noticed until he had it in his hands. The wild part of his mind was shouting, *Shoot!* But the cool part was remembering another time he had fired a single shot in the air and then was helpless.

But in the end none of it made any difference. When Bonny grabbed for his gun, the choice was taken out of Arnie's hands. With the briefest breath of a sigh, he added the least bit of pressure to the trigger. The shotgun roared.

A path of blood and destruction opened in front of the shotgun's muzzle. Arnie was appalled and stunned. Bonny fell back with a smear of crimson where his face had been. The wild part of Arnie's mind shouted, *He's dead! I killed him!* The cool part of his mind whispered, *Follow it up fast, before they have a chance to strike back!*

He let go of the now useless shotgun and dived for the revolver Bonny had dropped in falling. But the scene was frozen in his mind. The shotgun, loaded with buckshot, had left Bonny without a face. One or two other scavengers had reeled back grabbing at bleeding parts of their bodies. Frank Carr had lunged halfway up from the counter, and there he hung, as if suspended on wires, his left arm hanging useless and dripping bright red blood on the floor.

That was the scene that Arnie saw—eerily silent and still, as if they had all been instantly frozen in a huge block of ice—as he grabbed up the dead man's revolver and began shooting wildly.

Someone howled in pain or rage. The scavengers stampeded like cattle in a thunderstorm. By the time Arnie fired the last shot in Bonny's revolver, the store was clear of scavengers. Live scavengers, anyway.

Arnie fell against the counter where Frank Carr had been sitting. The wildness in his brain was still shouting, *Shoot! Shoot!* But there was nobody else to shoot at. Nobody else to kill. Still, the voice would not be silent. He stumbled to the firearms case, selected an ugly little American Bulldog revolver, and made sure it was loaded. He got another shotgun and loaded it with buckshot. He acted calmly and coolly, as if he did this sort of thing every day.

Outside, several horses were already fogging it away from the store. Scavengers, Arnie thought to himself, are not soldiers. Not fighters. They are just what they call themselves, scavengers. "Well," he said aloud, glancing down at Bonny, "there's one less of you today."

Now that the moment of violence was over, the wildness inside him receded. He walked dumbly through the wreckage of his store. Strangely, he was not frightened. He had seen the putty faces fleeing in panic. He walked around aimlessly for what seemed like a long time, picking up broken pieces of stock, putting them down again. There was something inside him waiting to be let out, but it was in no hurry. It sat there in some dark place, waiting patiently.

"Boy, you hear me in there?"

Arnie was startled at the sound of Frank Carr's voice. He hurried to the back door, the shotgun at his shoulder. "Get away from here, Carr. Consider yourself lucky I don't shoot you."

"I want my brother. I don't aim to leave without him."

Arnie thought for a moment. The dead youth

called Bonny was the brother of the scavenger leader. Somehow this possibility had not occurred to him before. He pressed flat against the wall and quietly scanned the area around the blacksmith shed. Besides Carr there were only two scavengers left. Carr's arm was still dangling at his side. Still bleeding.

"I ain't leavin' here without my brother, boy."

"Your brother's dead," Arnie called.

"I know that."

Arnie stepped away from the door and slid into a corner of the store, behind the meat box. "All right, you and the two others come get him. Leave your guns on the ground outside the door. I've got a shotgun."

He heard them tramping up the steps to the loading platform. Carr entered the store, trailing a bright string of blood. He didn't speak, and he didn't look around for Arnie. He went to his brother and looked down at the still body. "Fred, you and Hubie come in here and carry him out for me."

The two remaining scavengers came into the store and picked up the body and carried it out. Frank Carr stood for a moment doing nothing. At last he said, "I'll be comin' back, boy. A Carr always pays what he owes. And I owe you for Bonny." Without ever looking at Arnie, he turned and walked out.

Arnie stayed where he was until he heard the

horses leaving the store yard. Then he went to a window and saw four horses entering a thicket of post oaks. One of the animals carried the body of Bonny Carr face down across the saddle.

Arnie began to sweat. His hands, which had been so steady, began to tremble. He went to the firearms case and put the shotgun and pistol away. His mouth was dry and his insides were cold. For a long while he wandered about in the wreckage, always careful to go around the bloody spot on the floor where Bonny Carr had fallen.

He picked up a piece of what had once been a good German razor. One of the scavengers had broken the blade out of the handle, then he had broken the bright steel blade itself. "Now why would a man do a thing like that?"

He waded through a pile of spilled canned goods and a tangle of unwound muslin. He looked at Purdy's heavy leatherbound books. "Looks like the joke's on you, Harve. The store's gone bust without any help from you at all." He even managed a bitter grin.

But the coldness in his guts was spreading. The thing inside him began to stir. It wanted out. "I know what it is," he said aloud. "It ain't the store— I don't give a damn about that."

He had killed a man. That was the thing that had to be let out. "Lord," he said appalled, "I think I'm goin' to be sick."

CHAPTER EIGHT

Arnie was sitting in front of the store, on the porch, when Amy Hall and her father pulled up in the Hall farm wagon. Amy was smiling but seemed slightly nervous. She called to Arnie, but he only sat there and looked at them.

Andrew Hall and his daughter got down from the wagon and came across the store yard. Hall, a stooped, colorless man, like most of the farmers in the post oaks, shot an uneasy look at his daughter. "He don't look right to me."

He didn't look right to Amy either, but she didn't say so. She stopped in front of Arnie and said, "I've been thinkin' about the sewin' machine and makin' shirts, like we talked about. I know you promised to get Abe Cutter to bring the machine out to the place, but I thought I could get started sooner if I got Pa to . . ." Her voice trailed off. "Arnie, are you all right?"

Arnie looked at his hands. They were still trembling. At last he cleared his throat and said, "It wasn't in my head to kill him. I don't know. They was breakin' up everything and I was mad. I told them to stop. And they wouldn't. And all the time they was laughin' fit to bust a gut. Then the gun went off."

Amy's face had gone almost white. "What is it, Arnie? Who did you kill?"

"Name of Bonny. That's all I know. Scavengers."

Suddenly she understood. "Where are they now?"

"Gone. They took Bonny and throwed him across his saddle and lit out. But they'll be back."

"How do you know?"

"I know."

Amy looked at her father. "Pa, look in the store and see what it's like."

Andrew Hall rubbed a nervous hand over his face. "I don't know. Scavengers. Maybe we ought to get away from here."

"They won't be back so soon. Not if one of them is dead." Amy gestured impatiently. "Go on now. I want to talk to Arnie."

Cautiously, Andrew Hall advanced to the front door and peered inside. He groaned—partly in dismay at the wreckage, partly in relief at seeing no scavengers there. His daughter sat down beside Arnie. "How long's it been?" she asked.

Wearily, Arnie shook his head. "I ain't sure. I kind of lost track of time."

"Was it this mornin'?"

He nodded. "They shot the lock off the back door. That was the thing that woke me up."

"How many was there of them?"

"Fourteen, I think. I recollect countin'. Carr. That was the leader's name."

Something happened to Amy Hall's face. It became stiff and expressionless. "Frank Carr?"

166

"I think so. Bonny was his kid brother. I killed him."

"Set still a minute," Amy told him. She got up and went into the store. When she came back she had a tin cup full of Maryland whisky. She looked shaken.

"Did you see the blood?" Arnie asked bleakly.

"Pa's cleanin' it up. Here, take some of this."

Automatically, Arnie took the cup. "The whisky barrel," Amy said bitterly. "One of the few things they didn't break up."

Arnie drank the whisky as if it had been water. His insides churned. But pretty soon the whisky started to take hold. He looked at Amy and smiled bitterly. "I guess I've been actin' pretty much the fool."

"You've been actin' normal. You've been knocked on the head, and kicked, and you've killed a man. It's enough to make anybody feel queer for a while."

"Bonny Carr was his name."

"Frank Carr's brother," she said coldly. "I've heard about them. Scavengers, like you say. Headquarters up in the Indian Territory some-wheres. Sometimes they range into Arkansas, but this is the first time I know about them comin' down into Texas. You never heard about the Carr brothers?"

Arnie shook his head painfully.

"No reason why you should. They ain't the kind

to mess with cowmen, or anybody else that's apt to put up a fight. Country stores and small farm settlements, that's the kind of place they mostly favor. The post oaks and the piney wood country has been plagued with their kind ever since hard times hit." She breathed deeply. "Well, it's over now. They won't be comin' back."

"Frank Carr said he'd be back."

"They never come back," Amy insisted, "to any place that shows the spunk to fight them."

Arnie pushed himself up from the porch. Sooner or later he would have to look at the store again.

He walked to the open doorway and groaned to himself. It looked even worse than he had remembered; if there was a single item on the ground floor that was not broken or damaged, he did not see it. Mentally, he composed a letter to the lawyer in Placer.

Dear Lawyer Webber, You can have this store and welcome to it I wouldn't take the goddam place if you was to beg me I am sick of it and I quit so never mind tryin to locate a buyer. . . .

Amy Hall looked at him and said brightly, "It ain't so bad. It could be a lot worse."

"How?" Arnie asked bitterly.

"Well, all these bolts of cloth, for one thing. They ain't a complete loss. You can mark it down and the farm wives will buy it; they can wash it and mend it and make dresses out of it. I could still use most of the striped hickory for makin' shirts. Wash it first, and cut the patterns around the parts that's torn." She waded through the rubble, past the large wet spot on the floor where Andrew Hall had cleaned up the blood. "Most of the heavy things are all right. The plows and planters and things like that—there ain't hardly any way you can break iron. They're just thrown around every which way, that's all." Suddenly she stopped. Her mouth fell open in alarm. "The sewin' machine!"

She flew up the stairs and Arnie followed dumbly. The heavy machine had been knocked over, the pulley belt broken, bobbin and needles scattered all over—but the machine itself seemed to be in one piece. She breathed a heavy sigh of relief and smiled up at Arnie. "See, things ain't as bad as you thought."

Arnie could hardly see how they could be worse, although admittedly the second-floor damage was not as bad as that below. Amy got up off her knees and looked at him worriedly. "Arnie, you do believe everything's goin' to be all right, don't you?"

"I don't believe anything will ever be all right," Arnie said harshly. "Not here. Not in these damn post oaks. I don't know why I haven't pulled my stake and left. If I had a decent horse to ride, that's what I'd do right now." He wheeled and tramped back down the stairs.

"Ain't much more we can do here today," Andrew Hall said as Arnie came back down to the first floor. "Tomorrow we'll get some help and put things straight. It won't be so bad."

"You can set a match to the place, for all I care!" Arnie snarled. He stopped just long enough to fill a tin cup with whisky. He tramped across the store yard to the blacksmith shed, and there he sat beside the cold forge for a long while, sipping the raw whisky and simmering in his own bile.

Amy Hall opened the back door and started toward the blacksmith shed, but her father took her arm and held her with unaccustomed firmness. "Let him be. The boy's got some decidin' to do, and I don't figger he wants folks tellin' him how to do it."

Amy looked startled, but after a moment she allowed herself to be led back inside the store. After a while they left by the front way and Arnie heard the wagon rattle onto the road and head toward Oak College.

The rest of the day passed in a leaden haze. Arnie returned to the store several times to refill his cup at the whisky barrel, but he made no effort to put some sort of order to the wreckage. Finally he fell asleep in the blacksmith shed, wondering fuzzily if he could sell himself a ticket on the next west-bound stage. Considering the condition of the store, he wasn't sure the stage company would accept a ticket from there.

He woke up the next morning with a sore head

and a stiff back and a great, cold emptiness in his gut. The gray, sad figure of Matt Loving was standing over him. With some difficulty Arnie pushed himself to a sitting position and reached for the tin cup. It was empty.

"I guess you seen the store."

The preacher-clerk nodded. "Miss Amy told me what happened. But it ain't so bad—things can be set straight."

"Don't bother," Arnie groaned. "Not on my account." He limped across the store yard and went into the store long enough to fill the cup. The whisky tasted like coal oil, but he drank it. He looked around until he found a bottle of electric bitters that hadn't been broken; he emptied the bitters on the floor and filled the bottle with bourbon.

"Mr. Smith," Loving started as Arnie came back out of the store.

"Matt," Arnie told him harshly, "whatever you got to say, if it's about the store, I don't want to hear it. I'm sick of the store. Tell you the truth, I'm a little sick of you too." Raw whisky on an empty stomach. He realized that he was drunk.

He wandered across the hitching ground and into a post oak thicket. The long-faced clerk watched him sadly but did not try to stop him. Arnie kept going, blundering through the scrub timber, until the store was out of sight. He didn't know where he was going, and he didn't care, just so he didn't have to look at that store any more.

From time to time he would pull the cork on the bitters bottle and take a drink of bourbon. His legs became rubbery. His stomach heaved. From time to time he would glimpse Bonny Carr's startled face, just before the buckshot tore it away. Then he would take another drink of whisky.

"Arnie Smith," he heard himself saying, "you're a sorry sight to see, and that's a fact. What you done you done because you never had any say about it. It was him or you. Put it out of your head."

Easier said than done. He walked for what seemed to be a long time. Finally he came to a creek and washed his face and drank some water. It didn't make him feel any better.

He fully realized that he was acting the fool, but that didn't seem to matter. What did anything matter? He had lost the store and he didn't even have the money to go look for another job, and he had killed a man. It had been a big day. A day to remember. He stumbled into a wild plum thicket and fell down and went to sleep.

Some time later he came awake with a big hand shaking him. "Come alive, boy. The day's almost over, and there's still plenty to do." It seemed to Arnie that he had been through all this before. Cautiously, he opened his eyes. He looked up at the big, wryly grinning face of Robert Wakefield Hefford, the gun drummer.

"Where did *you* come from?"

"The store. A clerk there said you'd took a bottle

of bitters and was blunderin' about in the thickets. Damn fool way for a man to act, if you was to ask me."

"I didn't ask you."

Bob Hefford laughed. "Still got some vinegar left in you. Good. From the looks of that store, you'll need it."

Arnie sat up and held his aching head. "Where'd you come from? Besides the store, I mean."

The gun drummer shrugged. "Just happened to be travelin' these parts and heard about the scavengers. Hard news travels fast." He picked up the bitters bottle and sniffed it. "Not bad bourbon, if I'm any judge. But it ain't goin' to settle your troubles for you. That's one thing I know about."

"I got a preacher clerkin' for me at the store," Arnie told him harshly. "When I want to hear a sermon I'll hear it from him."

Hefford grinned and refused to take offense. "That preacher ain't had the close acquaintance with Maryland Bourbon that I have." He hunkered down, with his back against a sapling, and carefully lit a crooked cigar. Suddenly he looked tired, and older than his years. "I hear you killed a man."

Arnie glared at him but said nothing.

"It ain't a light load to carry, knowin' you sent a man to kingdom come. But what comes in a bottle don't make it any lighter—I've got some reason to know."

Arnie was sick. He was in no mood for diplomacy. "The last time I seen you, you didn't seem to think so."

Hefford laughed without changing his solemn expression. "Do like I say, not like I do. Ain't that the way the sayin' goes?" Hefford puffed placidly on his cigar. "I take it," he said at last, "that you don't aim to spend the rest of your life blunderin' around in these thickets. Just what *do* you aim to do with yourself?"

"There ain't but one thing. Strike back west and hook up with a cow outfit."

"What about the store?"

"There ain't any store. Not after the scavengers got finished with it."

Hefford waved the thought away with his cigar. "Even if it's as bad as you think, it's still worth somethin'. The location and the building. The land and cotton your uncle took on debts. Someday it'll be worth plenty."

"I don't aim to wait. I've had a bait of this place. Anyhow . . ."

Hefford's eyebrows pointed up slightly.

With a sigh of resignation, Arnie told the gun drummer about Purdy. And the heavy debts that stood against the store. And the accounts that were collectable only in land, if they were collectable at all.

Unmoved, Hefford heard him out. "Still, it would be worth somethin' to somebody. The price of a good horse and rig, and maybe a stake to see you to your next job. But not if you just walk off and leave it. You got to give the lawyer a chance to locate a buyer."

"He's had his chance. There ain't any buyers."

"There's always buyers for land, if the price is right."

Arnie shrugged. He didn't feel strong enough to argue. "There's still Purdy to contend with. You can't keep a store from goin' under without a book-keeper."

Hefford smiled in a strange way. "Maybe Purdy will change his mind about comin' back." He tossed his cigar. Then, with surprising strength, he took Arnie's arm and pulled him upright. "Walk," he ordered quietly. "It'll do you good."

Arnie was soon gasping for breath, but Hefford kept him going with timely nudges in the small of his back. Arnie didn't know where they were going, he didn't even know in what direction they were traveling. Then, without warning, they broke out of a thicket and there was the store.

There must have been a dozen wagons pulled up on the hitching ground. Arnie scowled at Hefford, but the gun drummer only smiled. Arnie allowed himself to be nudged across the store yard and through the back door. He rubbed his eyes. Most of the litter had been swept up and carried away. Tables had been set upright, bolts of cloth had been carefully brushed and rewound. Shelves had been nailed back on the wall, and stock that was still usable was back in place.

Several sodbusters looked up as Arnie and Hefford came through the back door, then they went on with cleaning the store. Arnie recognized most of them—some of them were the ones who had pulled him down from the porch and stomped him.

He walked slowly toward the middle of the store. The spot where Bonny Carr had fallen was scrupulously clean; the floor had been scrubbed white with lye water. Arnie climbed the stairs to the second floor and found a group of women, Amy Hall among them, setting things right. When he went down again there was bewilderment in his face.

Bob Hefford grinned. "What's the matter, boy, you look a mite queer."

"Not long ago these men was haulin' me down on the ground and kickin' me."

"The world's full of surprises," the gun drummer said philosophically.

Arnie withheld comment on that and continued his inspection of the store. "It's still a mess, in spite of all the work. It'll take a week just to figger out what the loss is—and even if I got it figgered out, it wouldn't do any good. Without a bookkeeper."

The farmers who had been working quietly all day now began to break up and drift away. Arnie didn't know what to say to them, so he didn't say anything. He found an undamaged nail keg and sat on it, too tired to move. It occurred to him that he hadn't eaten for almost two days, but he wasn't hungry. The whisky barrel was within easy reach, but he didn't want that either.

The store, cast in the harsh light of a coal oil lamp, was as silent as a graveyard. It might as well *be* a graveyard, Arnie thought, for all the good it is to anybody. He found himself staring at the bleached spot on the floor. It didn't occur to him to wonder what had happened to Hefford.

He sat there listening to the sounds of the night and thinking nothing. Minutes became hours. Then, somewhere in the darkness, he heard a two-horse team jolting over the country road. He knew, without actually thinking about it, that it was Bob Hefford returning from wherever it was that he had vanished to.

The heavy buggy rattled alongside the store and came to a stop. In a few minutes Hefford appeared in the back doorway. "Well, now," he said, looking enormously pleased with himself, "she don't look so bad, does she? Now that you got her cleaned up some."

Arnie was still slumped over on the keg. "Where've you been?"

"I been havin' a talk with Harve Purdy."

This bit of information penetrated Arnie's almost overpowering lethargy. "Talk about what?"

"About the store, and how it ought to be kept

open. About clerkin', and bookkeeping, and such." Hefford lit a cigar and flipped the match into the sandbox next to the stove. "He's a tough nut, old Harve is. But when everything's said and done, he'll come around and listen to reason."

Arnie sat very still. He could see Harve Purdy listening to reason. Bob Hefford's brand of reason rode in a cutaway holster just beneath his left arm. "What did Harve say?"

"About what I expected he'd say. He's comin' back. Trouble is, boy, you don't know how to handle high-strung old geezers like Harve. Hit him the wrong way and he turns stubborn as a Kansas mule—but that's over and forgot now."

"Did you threaten to shoot him if he didn't come back?"

The gun drummer laughed. "Boy, I'm afraid you've got a suspicious mind. Like I told you, it was pure reason." Hefford looked at his cigar. "I offered him an interest in the store. He wanted half. I offered him ten per cent. We finally settled on twenty."

For a moment Arnie was stricken dumb. Then he hollered, "Twenty per cent of the store! You're out of your head!"

But the gun drummer would not be ruffled. "I told Harve you wouldn't likely understand. Not right at first."

"I won't *never* understand!" Arnie hollered in outrage. "What right have you got to give away twenty per cent of my store?"

"A little while ago," Hefford went on calmly, "you were ready to pick up and quit the place like she sat. Now you got yourself in a steam because you stand to lose twenty per cent of it. That don't make sense, boy."

"I don't care if it makes sense or not!" Arnie heard his voice going shrill. He had been through too much these past two days; he was getting as excitable as a schoolgirl. With a great deal of effort he reined himself in and pulled his voice back to normal. "All right. Maybe it don't make sense. But this is still my store, and I can do anything I want to with it."

"Do you want eighty per cent of the store that Purdy can keep runnin', or a hundred per cent of a store that's goin' bust?"

"I don't give a damn!"

"That," the gun drummer observed, "is what you keep on sayin'. But you're still here, workin' and tryin' to make a go of it."

Arnie flushed. "I'd trade the whole shootin' match for a single shot saddle!"

"Boy, I don't like to bring it to your attention this way, but you're a liar. You've been a cowhand all your life and you know what it's like to be a nobody. Now you've got a store and stand to amount to somethin'. Nobody but a fool would let a chance like that get away from him."

This thought brought Arnie up short for a moment. He glared angrily at the gun drummer.

"There's somethin' else to be considered," Hefford went on. "Purdy had good reason to think the store would go to him when your uncle passed on. He's worked here most of his life. Worked as hard as your uncle did. He figgers the place is his by rights—part of it, anyhow. Tell you the truth, boy, I agree with him."

Arnie looked at him sullenly. "That wasn't the way my uncle saw it."

"Your uncle was as mean as a she-coyote with a hole full of pups. I ain't surprised that he passed Purdy over in his will. But I was sort of hopin' you'd want to do somethin' to set it right."

"All I want is to sell out and get away from here."

"Then you better give Harve his share. He's the only one that can keep it runnin' until you locate a buyer."

These new thoughts were racing in circles in Arnie's mind. The idea of parceling the store out in shares in order to keep it going had never occurred to him. "How do I know twenty per cent of the store would satisfy him? Why didn't he ask me for it, if that's what he wanted?"

"Because Harve's a prideful man. He couldn't let you think he was beggin' for somethin' he figgers is rightfully his."

Arnie found this kind of talk frustrating and aggravating and he wanted to get away somewhere and think about it quietly. "I'll think about it," he said grudgingly. "I'll go to Placer and talk it over with Webber."

"Tomorrow?"

"All right. Tomorrow." He made a weary sound.

"There's one more thing I haven't mentioned yet." Hefford studied the tip of his cigar and pretended not to hear Arnie groan. "You're goin' to be needin' another clerk. I'm puttin' in for the job."

Arnie looked shocked. "The store's got all the clerks it can use. Besides, you've got a job sellin' guns. What do you want with a clerkin' job in a country store?"

"Say I'm sick of travelin'." Hefford sighed faintly. "It ain't like you'd be gettin' a green hand. On Saturdays I could keep the hotheads from gettin' too rowdy—you'd be surprised how peaceful it would be, with a gun slinger around." He flipped his burnt-out cigar to the sandbox. "Anyhow, I was talkin' to Lovin', and he's got a preachin' job at a protracted camp meetin' in Placer. He's been tryin' to figger out a way to tell you."

Arnie's head throbbed. His mouth tasted like gunpowder. He lurched to his feet, not wanting to talk or think any more about the store.

Hefford said, "And there's the scavengers to think about."

Arnie looked at him dully. "What about them?"

"You killed Frank Carr's brother. He'll be comin' back. One dark night he'll be layin' for you in a thicket with a shotgun. Or some mornin' you'll open the door to the store and there he'll be. When that happens it might not be a bad notion to have a gun slinger handy."

An icy finger went up Arnie's back. He didn't want to think about Frank Carr and the scavengers. Not now, with Bonny's dead face still fresh in his memory. Tomorrow. He would talk to the lawyer and think it all out, tomorrow. "Have you got a place to sleep?" he asked the gun drummer.

"Anywhere my team stops, that's home to a travelin' man."

Arnie made a helpless gesture with one hand. "Throw your bed in the shed room."

CHAPTER NINE

Herbert Webber groaned to himself when he saw Arnie getting off the southbound stage in Placer. The trouble with young folks, they expected results in a hurry. Results, as Webber knew too well, came with painful slowness, if at all, when your business was selling country stores in times of tight money.

He was pleasantly surprised when Arnie failed to mention the subject as soon as he entered the office. "Mr. Webber," the young store owner asked without preamble, "how well do you know Harve Purdy?"

Webber blinked his owl-like eyes. "Very well. As I believe I mentioned once before."

"What would you say if I gave him twenty per cent of the place? Would that hobble you in tryin' to find a buyer?"

The lawyer showed his amazement. For a long while he had been mildly outraged that Syrus Smith had left Purdy no part of the store in his will. "Good bookkeepers are hard to come by," he said cautiously. "A prospective buyer would most likely be glad to make Mr. Purdy a part of the bargain."

Arnie sat back in relief. "That's what I wanted to know." Then at some length he explained his situation while Webber listened with growing wonder and a surprising amount of understanding. "I consider your plan a wise one in every respect," the lawyer said, when Arnie had finished. "I'll get the papers drawn up right away, if that's what you want."

"It ain't what I want," Arnie said, with a return to bitterness. "But Purdy's got me where the hair's short, and he knows it. So I got to make the best of a bad bargain." He slumped in his chair. "I figgered that much out after the scavengers left."

"Scavengers?"

Arnie told him about Frank Carr and his bunch. Herbert Webber looked dazed. "Were the store's books lost or damaged in any way?"

"Everything else, just about, but not them damn books."

The lawyer patted his forehead in obvious relief.

"Well, then the sale of the store won't be affected to any important degree. Your part of it, that is."

Arnie's feeling of mild elation passed quickly on the silent streets of Placer. He rambled dispiritedly from one blank-faced store to another, laboriously killing time until he could catch the next north-bound stage to Smith. The heady smell of chili and frying steaks spiced the air around a frame shack calling itself the Placer Café. On the opposite side of the street a saloon sign beckoned. But café grub and saloon whisky were not for the likes of Arnie Smith, with no money in his pockets.

At the end of the street a scaling sign waved forlornly in front of a leather goods store. *Calab McPhitter. Doctor.*

Doctor of what, it did not say. Arnie looked at the sign for some time. In his mind he saw Sam Tillman, the laudanum drinker—he recalled that McPhitter had been Tillman's doctor. Then he remembered something else—children with hot eyes and sweaty faces and knobby limbs. On sudden impulse he climbed the outside stairway and opened the door to the doctor's office.

Calab McPhitter sat tilted back in a yellow oak chair, his feet propped on a roll-top desk, reading a book. "Sit down," he said, without looking up. "I'll be with you in a minute." At last McPhitter reached the end of a paragraph, held his place with the tip of a dirty finger, and glanced briefly at his visitor. "Sit down, sit down, this won't take long." He continued his reading. Arnie cleared some newspapers from a cane-bottom chair and sat down. He built a cigarette, lit it, smoked it, and stamped it out on the floor. McPhitter turned a page. From time to time he would grunt in agreement with what he was reading.

Arnie occupied himself with studying the man, Calab McPhitter, and his office, at first glance, was little more than a trash heap with a few pieces of furniture moved in. Ancient newspapers and magazines littered the floor. Books overflowed the wall shelves and lay in untidy piles on the desk. A small glass-fronted case with a few bottles in it stood near the doorway—this small case, it appeared, contained McPhitter's entire stock of medical equipment and supplies.

Arnie turned his attention to the man himself and what he saw was not encouraging. McPhitter was a gaunt cadaver of a man with dirty, clawlike hands and a scraggly beard. He wore cheap jean pants and a hickory shirt, both items the worse for wear and filthy. Arnie squinted hard at the cover of the book that McPhitter was reading. *Essay on Criticism.* He had never heard of it.

He looked at some of the other books that lined the walls and cluttered the floor. *Pleasures of Hope* by Thomas Campbell. *The Duty of Civil Disobedience* by Henry David Thoreau. *Impressions and Comments* by Havelock Ellis. Nothing there that Arnie had ever heard of.

Suddenly McPhitter looked up and laughed with the dryness of dead leaves rustling. "The bookful blockhead, ignorantly read, with loads of learned lumber in his head."

Arnie looked at him blankly.

"Alexander Pope," McPhitter explained. Then he sighed, fumbled a cigar out of his shirt pocket, and lit it. "I don't suppose you're acquainted with Alexander Pope, are you, young man?"

"I don't think so."

The doctor sighed again. "Too bad. Well," he said with sudden impatience, "what do you want? You don't want a purgative, do you? I don't see any cuts or bullet wounds or broken bones. What is it?"

Arnie was on the brink of mentioning Sam Tillman, the laudanum drinker, but changed his mind at the last moment. "I come to ask about some children."

McPhitter glanced at his book. He looked bored. "What children? What about them? Are they sick?"

"They ain't in bed sick, if that's what you mean. I don't know—they just look mighty peaked. Run down, kind of, like they was half starved. Ribs stickin' out, arms and legs like matchsticks but knobby at the joints."

"Rickets," McPhitter said uninterestedly. "White diet."

Arnie blinked. "White diet?"

"Steady feed of fat pork and corn bread. I've told

186

the fools that a diet like that will kill them, but they won't listen."

"These rickets," Arnie asked, "can a body cure hisself of them?"

The doctor shot him a look of faint and fleeting interest. "You look kind of young to be having kids with or without rickets."

"They ain't my kids. They're kids that belong to farm families up in the north part of the county. It's just a thing I got to thinkin' about, so I thought I'd ask."

McPhitter cracked his book and quickly read a few sentences. "Fresh vegetables," he said shortly. "They'll help. But they won't cure rickets. Takes fish oil for that. Oil from the liver of the codfish is best, if you can get it."

"Where does a body get this fish oil?"

The doctor spread his hands in a gesture of helplessness.

"There used to be some at the store here in Placer, but they ran out and never reordered." He opened his book again. "Is that all you wanted?"

"I guess so." Arnie pushed himself up from the chair. "Except for one thing. I ain't got any money to pay you."

"It's a dollar. Hand it to me when you can." The doctor turned his back to his caller and returned to the brilliant world of Mr. Alexander Pope.

Arnie spent a restless night in the seed house and caught the next northbound stage to Smith. The driver looked at him curiously. "Didn't I haul you this way once before?"

"I wish you hadn't," Arnie told him bitterly. "It's the worst thing that ever happened to me, and that's a fact."

After a night in the seed house, the bubble of youth lay still and sour within him. A sense of cold reality clamped to his body like a set of iron shackles. "I let a gun shark and a crooked book-keeper talk me out of twenty per cent of my store!" he thought. "Arnie Smith, you ain't got the sense of a spotted bronc in the springtime!"

The last thing Herbert Webber had told him before he left Placer was, "Don't lose heart, Mr. Smith. I'll find you a buyer before long."

"How long?" Arnie had asked wearily.

"There's always more money around in the fall of the year. By Christmas time, I'd say, you ought to have the place off your hands."

Christmas time. It might as well have been the turn of the century, as far as Arnie was concerned.

"Here you are," the driver hollered. "Smith Station."

Arnie climbed out of the coach and tramped across the dusty hitching ground. "It ain't much of a home," he thought with little consolation, "but at least it's a place to come to when there ain't nowhere else."

A wagon was pulling away from the store. The farmer gave Arnie a friendly wave as he turned onto the rutted road. Arnie wondered bleakly if he was one of the bunch that had pulled him off the porch that day. It was hard to tell. After a while all sodbusters started to look alike.

He climbed the steps to the porch and stood for a moment in the doorway. The smell of the place had already become a familiar one to him. He breathed it in—coffee and vinegar and block salt and feed. Leather and wood and painted iron. Sizing on the bolts of cloth, the musty wool-and-cotton smell of jeans. Coal oil, whisky, molasses. Lye soap that had been used to clean up Bonny Carr's blood. Like it or not, it had become a part of him now.

He looked the place over carefully. Shelves, he noted, were back on the wall. Stock was in place. The wreckage had been straightened out and the litter swept outside. It was beginning to look like a store again.

Harve Purdy was back in his old place behind the grilled post office window. He watched Arnie with suspicious eyes and a pulled-down mouth.

Arnie said, "The lawyer's drawin' up the papers, Harve. You got what you wanted."

Harve's grim mouth relaxed a little, but not much. "It ain't more'n right. Anybody'll tell you."

"I ain't arguin'. I'm too tired to argue." He went back to the medicine section and searched the shelves carefully. There seemed to be a good supply of Phyto-Gingerin, Oxien, and Kodol Dyspepsia Cure. Not even Frank Carr's dedicated store wreckers had managed to break all of the bottles of Electric Bitters, Dr. Shoop's Restorative, and McLean's Strengthening Cordial. There were a great many bottles of Dr. Pierce's Favorite Prescription, powerfully laced with tincture of opium and digitalis. Dozens of cans and boxes of powders and herbs. Almost half a case of McGill's Nerve Food and One Minute Cough Cure. There were powders and ointments and liquids and compounds guaranteed to cure headaches, fullness in the head, shooting pains, dizziness, dots before the eyes, dyspepsia, and constipation. There was castor oil, oil of anise, oil of cloves, and electric oils for rubbing away soreness and aches. But fish liver oil, Arnie could not find.

"While I was in Placer I got to talkin' to Doc McPhitter . . ."

"McPhitter's a quack," Harve Purdy snapped.

"Maybe. But he's got more books than I could count, and I figger he must of learned *some*thin' out of all that readin'." But Purdy's face had taken on that wooden look and Arnie knew that he would never be able to convince him there was anything good about McPhitter. "Why is it," he asked casually, "that the store don't stock cod liver oil?"

Purdy sniffed. "There ain't enough profit in it. We never stock it."

"We're goin' to start," Arnie said mildly. "Get an order wrote up tonight and get it off on the next stage." He quickly walked to the back of the store before the bookkeeper could start another argument.

• • •

July came and went almost without Arnie's noticing it. A welcome peace settled down around the Smith General Mercantile Company, and Arnie realized that it was largely due to Bob Hefford's quiet presence. There were no cutting scrapes or fights on store grounds while the former gun drummer was around. To Arnie's surprise, Hefford was also a good worker and—for the most part—sober.

July faded into August—hot and dusty days, the nights singing with millions of cicadas. Farm families were in the fields with their cotton sacks, and for a time the store became a deserted place. Even Matt Loving was gone—gone to his protracted camp meeting in Placer.

Long lines of cotton wagons labored over the rough country roads to the gins near Placer. Farmers had no time for Saturday gossip in the store yard—when they needed supplies they would send a field hand or a child to the store with a written order.

And every day the same arguments would arise between Arnie and the bookkeeper. "Fred Medder's over his credit limit," Harve Purdy would snap, glaring at a scribbled order as if it were poison. "He can't have this order of flour and bacon."

"A body can't pick cotton on an empty belly," Arnie would snap back. "Fill the order," he would tell Hefford.

Purdy's voice would grow shrill. "This store's part mine now! You got to listen to what I say!"

"When you own more of the store than I do, then I'll listen!"

In the end Fred Medder would get three pounds of flour instead of five, two pounds of dry salt meat where he had wanted four. By this loud and painful process, Arnie and his bookkeeper were slowly learning the art of compromise.

As August wore on a certain type of letter, addressed to the new owner of the Smith General Mercantile Company, began to arrive with depressing regularity. *Dear Sir: It has come to our attention that your account is thirty days overdue . . . realize it must be an oversight . . . Please remit promptly . . .*

Credit, as Arnie was learning, was a two-way proposition. "They're not goin' to stop sellin' us stuff, are they?" he asked in alarm.

"Not yet." Purdy shook his head grimly. "Not till the fall crop's in, and they know how we stand."

The bookkeeper was an old hand and knew what to do. He got out his old-fashioned quill pen, his tablet of coated paper, and wrote a long letter explaining in glowing detail how this was expected to be the best cotton season in the history of northeastern Texas, and how the store was on the soundest of financial ground and would be settling all its bills as soon as the crop was in.

"Is that the truth?" Arnie asked. "Are we goin' to settle our bills?"

"Some of them," Purdy said. "Enough to keep them from shuttin' off our stock. If we're lucky."

"And if we ain't lucky?"

"The banks will take over the store. Then they'll take over the farms that the store's got liens on. And we'll all be bust."

"Everybody but the banks."

Purdy looked at Arnie and his drawstring mouth twitched at the corners. For Purdy, that was the same as laughing out loud.

Behind all the bickering and worrying and hoping that they could somehow keep the place going until Christmas, business continued pretty much as usual. Amy Hall had started sewing together hickory shirts out of store cloth. Purdy gave his instant approval to the scheme when he heard about it. "Yes. That's good business. The store makes a profit on two items, the cloth and the shirts, instead of the shirts by theirselves. Besides that, it adds to the Hall credit limit. More profit to the store."

"Purdy, do you ever think about anything but this store?" Arnie asked.

The bookkeeper's mouth twitched for the second time in one day—a record. "Not much. You'll come to know how that can be someday. If you last."

"Just till Christmas time. After that, I never aim to think about a store again."

In July the shipment of garden seed had arrived and Arnie, over Purdy's bitter objections, had parceled them out among the farm families with children. "Shameful waste of good credit," Purdy sneered. "Cotton farmers ain't got the time to fool with vegetable gardens. And even if they did, it's too late for plantin'. And even if it wasn't too *late,* there'd have to be rain before anything could grow."

Arnie ignored him with a lordly order to Hefford. "See that these seeds gets to every family that's got kids. Put it on their bills, whether they want them or not."

Then, toward the middle of August, a minor miracle occurred. It rained. Not much—and weeks too late to help the cotton—but it did rain, enough to sprout vegetable seeds in the warm earth. As Arnie rode out on his Sunday rounds he saw the small patches of carrot tops, onions, greens, squash vines, and beans that were beginning to dot the reddish clearings. He would look at them and feel as proud as if he had personally done the planting and caused the rain.

When the shipment of cod liver oil arrived, it was the bitterness of the garden seed all over again. But in the end the oil reached the children, and Purdy grimly added it to the farmers' bills.

One day it occurred to Arnie that he hadn't set foot outside the store for four days, except to stagger to his sleeping room at night and fall into his bunk. "Hell and damnation!" he thought wearily. "What I need," he lectured himself, "is some sport for a change. See the sights. A place with some life to it, like Dodge or Ellsworth. I need to see some fancy dance-hall girls, and hear the wheel-of-fortune clickin', and taste myself some real saloon whisky."

What he had was a store—eighty per cent of a store—and a barrel of corn whisky that would rot the gizzard out of a coyote, and a little Maryland Bourbon that wasn't much better.

He lay in his bunk listening to the cicadas shrilling in the post oaks. "Boys," he suddenly announced to the boxlike room, "I've had about all of this country livin' that a body can take!"

He got up, pulled on his pants and shirt, and stamped into his high-top shoes. A big yellow moon lay over the thickets of scrub oaks—a harvest moon, he guessed. "Well, if I never seen another one, that'll be plenty soon enough for me!"

He opened the back door to the store and stumbled toward the shed room where Bob Hefford made his bed. "Hefford, you asleep?"

"I'm not asleep," the former gun drummer said quietly. He was not in the shed room. He was sitting on a goods case, next to the whisky barrel. Arnie struck a match and lit one of the coal oil lamps. Hefford had a tin cup in his hand and a faintly glazed look in his eyes. "Don't worry." He raised his cup and grinned faintly. "I'm keepin' track of what I drink. I'll put it on the books."

Arnie was mildly surprised to find Hefford drinking again, after several weeks of strict sobriety. He pulled up another goods box and drew a drink for himself from the bourbon keg. "A little somethin' to settle the dust." They saluted with their tin cups and drank.

Hefford slumped into a moody silence, staring into his cup. At last Arnie cleared his throat and asked, "Is somethin' the matter?"

"What started me back to the whisky barrel, you mean? That's a long story, boy." He helped himself to another drink. "The trouble with travelin'," he said at last, "is you meet too many folks that you'd just as soon never see again. The widow of a man you'd killed somewheres up the line. Maybe a brother, or mother, or sister. I figgered if I was to settle down and take a regular job, all that would be over and done with. But it ain't. I guess it's never done with all the way."

Arnie's stomach curled. He took another drink of whisky. "I know. I been doin' myself some thinkin' about Bonny Carr."

Hefford shrugged. "You're young. You'll get over it."

"Will I?"

The gun drummer looked at him steadily for a moment. "I figger you will. You'll have help."

Arnie sat back and looked surprised. "The only

help a cowhand gets is from hisself. And maybe from his horse, if he's got one."

Hefford allowed himself a small smile. "You're luckier'n most, boy. You got a woman—if you had sense enough to look around and see her."

Arnie's eyes widened. He didn't quite know whether to be amused or outraged. In the end he decided to pretend that he hadn't understood Hefford's words, and quickly changed the subject. "Talkin' about the Carrs—do you figger that Frank Carr will sure enough come back someday with that bunch of scavengers?"

"If you was Carr, what would you do? If Bonny had been your brother?"

Arnie sat for a moment in dejected silence. As the days had faded into weeks, his memory of the scavenger rampage had become faded. He had told himself that Carr would not attack the same place twice. Now he realized that it had been wishful thinking.

"You know somethin'?" he said at last.

"What?"

"I'm scared."

"Good. That means you've learned the biggest secret of stayin' alive."

It was a strange night—the two of them sitting there beside the whisky barrel, drinking some and talking a great deal.

"If Carr does come back with his bunch, ain't there somethin' we can do?"

"You can fight, like you did before."

"I don't know if I can. If it was to come down to shootin' another man, I ain't sure I could do it."

"You do what you have to do. That's somethin' you learn as you go along."

A strange night. As time went on Hefford became more and more distant. He would peer into the dark corners of the store and suddenly blink, as if he were seeing an old familiar ghost. After a while Arnie decided that he had had enough to drink and returned to his sleeping room.

Dry and dusty September fell and fluttered away, like so many pages from a calendar. By the end of the month it was obvious to everyone that the cotton crop was a failure. Gins that had often roared all the way through November, and sometimes up to Christmas time and past, were operating half-time by mid-October.

As October dragged into November Arnie more fully appreciated Purdy's rare abilities as a storekeeper. When a shipment of goods arrived from the railhead with a dray bill due, it was Purdy who somehow found the money to pay the wagoner and keep the goods from being returned to the supplier. If a customer was down with sickness, it was Purdy who discovered a way to extend his credit until he got on his feet again—usually at some other customer's expense and without interferring with his ironbound rules of bookkeeping. Arnie was satisfied in his own mind that there was something crooked in the way Purdy so casually adjusted balances and shifted debts from one side of the book to the other. But at least the place was still in business and Arnie knew without Purdy it would not have been.

Matt Loving's protracted meeting at Placer had been a great success. A shoe drummer reported seeing forty sinners at the mourners' bench one night. Somebody reported fifty baptizings in a cattle tank not far from the meeting grounds—which, everybody agreed, was something of a miracle in itself as the earthen tank, due to the long dry spell, held less than three feet of water in its deepest part. At any rate, Loving had established himself as a preacher of considerable persuasive gifts and had moved on to another meeting in another county.

Robert Wakefield Hefford had quietly moved in to take Loving's place in the store. Strangely enough, the three men, Hefford, Purdy, and Arnie, made a workable team. Hefford, wearing his gun slinger reputation like a concealed badge, managed by his presence to keep the place reasonably peaceful on Saturdays. At other times he was a steady worker. Occasionally there would be a pint or so of Maryland Bourbon on his personal account, which Purdy would grimly record in his books.

Arnie, in mysterious ways that he did not understand, had become something of a hero to some of his sodbuster customers. He had not asked for the honor and did not want it, but it was his all the same. Harve Purdy had fallen naturally and uncomplainingly into the role of the villain. When a customer's credit limit was suddenly slashed, it was Purdy's doing. While Arnie passed out bottles of cod liver oil and vegetable seeds, Purdy was denying them five pounds of flour and giving them three instead.

On one of those still, skin-prickling days of late November, soon after the first frost, Arnie found a small brown paper parcel on the dry goods counter. "Where did this come from?"

Harve Purdy looked up from his books and said sourly, "Aram Plott brought it yesterday. It's for you."

Arnie opened the parcel cautiously, as though he suspected it of being a bomb. Instead, it was two dozen wild persimmons, small, gold in color, sweet from the touch of early frost. "Why would Aram Plott bring me a batch of persimmons?"

"I never asked, and he never said."

Bob Hefford was leaning in the shed room doorway, grinning crookedly. "Ain't Aram Plott the one you let have the madstone?"

Arnie didn't remember. For all he knew, Plott could have been one of the men who had pulled him off the porch that day and given him a good kicking. Maybe Plott's conscience was bothering him. More likely, he was hoping to soften Arnie up with a few persimmons and then ask for an extension of his credit.

But Aram Plott never did ask for more credit, and the puzzle was never satisfactorily solved in Arnie's mind.

Despite the poor cotton crop, November was a time of quietly desperate activity in the store. Purdy worked late almost every night, poring over his books, writing letters, accepting cotton money from the farmers, reducing their debts on one hand and the store's debts on the other. In this silent, almost magical way, thousands of dollars changed hands without ten dollars of hard money ever seeing the cash box.

And there were decisions to be made. Most of them, in the matter of credit, were automatic. Purdy had reduced his system of bookkeeping to a set of hard and fast rules, and it was not often that the rules could be broken, if the system was to be allowed to stand.

One day Arnie came into the store to find Purdy gazing uncharacteristically into space. Then he shot a narrow look at Arnie. "What do you aim to do about Christmas?"

"Do about it?"

"I mean, what do you aim to do about the orderin'?"

Arnie didn't understand. Christmas in a cow camp was pretty much the same as any other day.

If you happened to be in town, it was an occasion for drinking red whisky until a marshal's deputy dragged you off to the calaboose. If they didn't have a calaboose, they locked you in a root cellar to sober up, or merely knocked you over the head with a pistol barrel and stretched you out in an alley.

"What does the store usually stock at Christmas time?"

The bookkeeper shrugged. "Oranges, apples, candy, for the young'uns. Dodads for the women, extra barrel of bourbon for the men."

Arnie was not very interested. He was still hoping to be somewhere else by that time. "You make out the order, Harve. But don't run the store in debt just so a bunch of sodbusters can do a whoop-de-doo at Christmas time."

"It's all high profit goods," Purdy told him superiorly.

Arnie had been through this before, and it made his head ache. The difference between the high profit goods and low profit goods was a slightly different figure in one column of Harve's books. To Arnie it was a matter that he found almost impossible to get serious about. To the bookkeeper it was as basic as life and death. "I leave it up to you," Arnie said wearily. And he went back to his sleeping room to write another letter to lawyer Webber.

CHAPTER TEN

The cotton season was over. In Placer the roar of the gins had been silenced. The clouds of reddish dust, stirred up by long trains of cotton wagons, had settled, leaving a ghostly shroud on the thickets of post oak.

The end of the ginning season was an anxious time for the farmers. It was a time for settling up debts and rearranging credit, and this year debts had grown and credit had shrunk. "The same with the store as it is with you," Arnie thought with dim bitterness. But sodbusters never thought about that. "All they think about is theirselves and tryin' to get their credit raised."

He was surprised to realize how close his thinking had come to that of his bookkeeper. He had been living with the store almost five months—it might have been five years, or five lifetimes. He could hardly remember a time when Arnie Smith was a carefree cowhand. That life and that time seemed as far away as it might have to a young reader of dime wild-Westerns in Brooklyn. He found himself staring into space and dreaming romantically of cow camp days—never mind the backbreaking work, the stench of cow chip fires, the gritty coffee, the half raw biscuits.

As November wore on he all but abandoned hope of ever selling the store and escaping the post oaks that he had come to despise. I'm stuck here, he thought dully, like a gnat to a smear of molasses. Hobbled and hamstrung, hog-tied by his debts to the wholesalers, just as the sodbusters were overwhelmed by their own debt to the store. It was a vicious, never-ending circle, and he never stopped being dismayed at finding himself caught in the middle of it.

On Sundays, when the weather allowed, he would ride out with Amy Hall looking at farms and wondering bleakly what they would be worth on the books of some bank in Boston or New York. This was something that he never completely understood—the financial chain that bound together and made partners of such unlikely people as Eastern bankers, land speculators, cotton speculators, wholesalers, storekeepers, farmers, right on down to the lowliest share cropper. He found it hard to believe that a Wall Street banker could care what happened to a sodbuster in the Texas post oaks. But Purdy assured him that they did.

On top of everything else, there was Amy Hall.

At odd and unexpected moments Arnie would find himself thinking about her. For unexplained reasons her face would suddenly flash in his mind. It was all very unsettling to a young man used to the raucous ways of a cowhand. Women, to a cowhand, usually meant a certain group of ladies known as fancy, in a certain kind of saloon or dance hall that catered to men who were free and had money to spend. The other kind of woman was of the type known as "decent." Decent women, as every cowhand knew, were to be avoided like range cows at horn fly time. This was a basic rule of survival. To ignore it was to invite disaster.

While standing on the store porch one day, staring blankly at the post oaks and hating them, Arnie suddenly thought about Stovepipe Harry Johnson. Stovepipe had been famous on the Western Trail. The saloons he had wrecked were legend; his barroom brawls folklore. Stovepipe was a man to be looked up to and admired. To be seen in his company was something a man could brag about for years to come.

And yet, even a man of Stovepipe's virtues had not been able to resist the ruinous attraction of a decent woman. Sold his saddle, got himself married, and hired on as a regular hand at a wagon yard. All in one disastrous year! His friends did not speak of him now, except in pity, or as an object lesson to the young.

Arnie was dumbly pondering the tragedy of Stovepipe Harry Johnson when the northbound stage lurched into view. The stagecoach, a mere speck at the point of a huge dust cloud, had become a symbol of escape for Arnie. "One of these days I'll write myself a ticket and get on that stage and never look back. If I had the sense of a snubbin' post," he muttered, "I'd do it today."

Accompanied by a good deal of profanity from

the driver, the four-horse team dragged the coach onto the store's hitching ground. The door opened and two men got out, weaving drunkenly from the rough ride.

One of the men, Arnie was surprised to see, was the lone surviving member of the Hinkle, Mawson, and Sylvester law firm, Herbert Webber. The other was a lean, unsmiling hawk of a man, garbed expensively in the hard gray worsted of an Eastern businessman or a high class gambler.

Arnie left the porch and walked across the store yard and shook hands with the lawyer. Webber was smiling widely and appeared highly pleased with the world in general. "Mr. Smith, shake hands with Mr. Devero. I expect you'll be pleased to hear that Mr. Devero is interested in buyin' the store from you."

Arnie was stunned. Just as he had about conditioned himself to the brutal fact that no man in his right mind—let alone with money in his pocket—would ever want to buy a country store, Webber was magically producing such a man. "I'm right proud to know you, Mr. Devero," Arnie told the stranger with a good deal of feeling.

He shook Devero's dry, talon-like hand. The longer Arnie looked at him the more hawklike he became—the quick dark eyes that seemed to bore in all directions at once, a narrow beak of a nose swooping down over colorless lips.

It was Arnie's opinion that the stranger didn't

look much like a country storekeeper. But he didn't dwell on it. Most likely storekeepers came in all sizes and styles, like anybody else.

Devero turned toward the store and fixed it with a jaded gaze. "I'd like to talk to the bookkeeper."

Arnie felt slightly lightheaded. There was an excited hammering in his chest. After all the waiting and hoping, here was finally a buyer!

There was an air of still expectancy inside the store. "Harve," Arnie said cautiously, "this here's Mr. Devero. He's thinkin' about buyin' my part of the store."

Purdy made no move to come out of his cubicle and shake hands. He sat behind the grilled window looking at the stranger with his usual sour expression. Devero looked back coolly. "I understand you own part interest in the store, Mr. Purdy."

"Part," Harve admitted grudgingly.

"Well, I'm sure we can come to a satisfactory understanding about that, if everything else is in order."

"My books are in order, if that's what you mean."

"I'm sure of it." Devero smiled faintly. It looked as if it pained him. "Well, Mr. Purdy, we might as well get started."

Arnie's ears began to ring, and then he discovered that he had been holding his breath in fear that Purdy would, out of pure contrariness, do something to ruin the bargain. But the bookkeeper merely shrugged his bony shoulders and began pulling down the heavy books and the goods boxes that he used as files.

The lawyer beamed at Arnie. "Mr. Smith, it seems to me that this is an occasion for a small celebration. It just happens that I brought something special up from Placer." He produced a flat bottle of aged Kentucky bourbon.

The two men left Purdy and Devero poring over the books and retreated to the shed room where quiet social drinking was usually done. "Here's to a profitable bargain for everybody concerned," Herbert Webber smiled, handing the bottle to Arnie.

They drank heartily from the pint bottle, and the velvety bourbon lay warm and soothing in Arnie's stomach. "How much do you reckon Devero's willin' to give for this place?"

"That'll depend on what he finds in the books," the lawyer said comfortably. "But don't you worry about the price, Mr. Smith. Everything'll be fair and square; I aim to see to that."

They took more drinks from the bottle. Then, in sudden alarm, Arnie said, "He *has* got the money, ain't he?"

The lawyer's expression turned curiously blank. "The men Mr. Devero represents have plenty of money, you can depend on that."

Robert Hefford appeared in the doorway of the shed room. "What bank does Mr. Devero represent?" He smiled blandly as the lawyer looked at him in astonishment. "If I ain't bein' too nosy."

"Bank? Who said anything about a bank?"

"Who else has got the cash for buying stores in times of tight money?"

Displeasure showed in Webber's eyes. "Of course Mr. Devero represents a bank—I thought that was understood. No one else would have the money; Mr. Hefford is entirely right about that." He glanced back at Hefford and smiled pleasantly enough. "It's the Cattlemen's State Bank at Fort Worth, to answer your question."

"How many other stores has the Cattlemen's State Bank at Fort Worth bought?" Hefford asked absently.

"I don't know. Several, I expect."

"How long do the stores generally stay in business after the bank takes over?"

Herbert Webber was beginning not to like the gun drummer or his questions. "May I ask what all this has to do with you, Mr. Hefford? You *are* only a clerk here. Or am I mistaken?"

Hefford took a cigar out of his vest pocket and carefully lit it. "You ain't mistaken." With a wide smile—like a smile cut into a paper mask—he nodded and moved back into the main room of the store.

Webber looked at the empty doorway for several seconds. "I must confess, Mr. Smith, that I never fully understood what caused you to hire a gunman to clerk in your store."

"He's a friend of mine," Arnie told him. A slight

frost seemed to settle on the warm bourbon cheer. They passed the bottle again, but their hearts were no longer in it. "What," Arnie asked, "did Hefford mean about stores stayin' in business?"

"Men like Robert Hefford, who have lived most of their lives on the edge of the law, are apt to mistrust an institution as solid and constructive as a bank."

Arnie shrugged. He didn't really care who Devero was or what kind of institution he represented, just so he had the cash and wanted to buy a country store.

Devero remained at the store for two days, bedding down with Hefford in the shed room. What the gun drummer and the banker had found to talk about those two nights, Arnie couldn't imagine.

On the third day Devero caught the southbound stage to Placer, burdened only with a small valise and two notebooks filled with figures. Arnie strongly suspected that the banker now knew a great deal more about the Smith General Mercantile Company than the present owner ever would. "I'll confer with my employers," Devero told Arnie before entering the coach. "When they make a decision, I'll let you know."

"How long am I supposed to set here waitin' for them to make a decision?"

Devero smiled his chilly smile. "Not long." The coach rattled off the hitching ground and onto the road. Arnie stood watching it until it disappeared in a boiling cloud of dust. He continued to watch until even the cloud of dust disappeared.

"Whoever you are," he muttered under his breath, "at the Cattlemen's State Bank at Fort Worth, hurry up and come to a decision and get me away from here!" It was about as close as he had ever come to praying.

December arrived in a driving rain. Day after day Arnie and Hefford and Purdy watched it come down in soaking torrents. "Goddamn the contrariness of Texas weather!" Purdy suddenly exploded. Arnie and Hefford looked at him as if he had suddenly gone mad. "Where was you in April when we needed you?" the bookkeeper hollered at the boiling clouds. Then he stomped off to his cubicle and worked on his books in grim silence.

On the fifth day the rain stopped. A cold sun came out and shone down on the shimmering bogs that passed as roads in northeast Texas. For almost a week the roads were all but impassable to farm wagons. The stagecoach was three days late, and the whip reported that he had never seen the creeks so high in wintertime.

For a week the world stopped. Smith, Texas, seemed to be slowly sinking into a sea of red mud. A lump as cold and hard as a bullet settled in the bottom of Arnie's stomach. This, he thought hopelessly, is the way it's goin' to be from now on. I ain't never goin' to get away from this place.

Nobody is goin' to buy it. Nobody is *crazy* enough to buy such a place!

Then one day he opened a mail sack and there was a letter from Webber. Dear Mr. Smith: *It is with considerable pleasure that I am now able to report . . .*

Arnie let out a whoop that brought Hefford out of the shed room in alarm. Purdy looked up from his precious books, scowling.

"They want the store! The bank wants it! They aim to buy it!" Excitedly, he read a little further. "Listen to this! '. . . agree to accept the liabilities of the Smith General Mercantile Company, as well as . . .' Here it is! '. . . in the amount of three thousand dollars . . .' *Three thousand dollars!* That's what they aim to pay me to take this place off my hands!"

He threw the letter into the air and danced a lively jig. "Three thousand dollars, free and clear! Did you hear that?"

Hefford and Purdy took the news with amazing calm. Purdy said a little grimly, "A bank never gets the worst of a bargain, don't you worry about that."

Hefford smiled faintly and said, "Well, it's a lot of money all right. Might even set you up in a little cattle business somewheres."

"*Any*wheres!" Arnie laughed. "Just so it ain't in these post oaks!" He gathered up the letter that he had flung in the air and finished reading it. "Listen to this, Purdy. They're willin' to buy your part too, if you want to sell."

The bookkeeper merely looked at him. "No. I won't sell."

"Purdy, you're loco. But that's your business." He went to the whisky barrel and drew a dram of Maryland Bourbon. "Boys, this here calls for a little celebration!" He passed the cup to Hefford and began drawing another for Purdy.

The bookkeeper clamped his jaws and shook his head. "I ain't a drinkin' man."

But Arnie was bubbling with excitement and good humor. "Purdy, you been between the shafts too long; you got to learn to enjoy yourself." He took the cup to the bookkeeper and shoved it through the opening in the grilled window.

But Purdy wouldn't touch it. "When a body fixes to sell his birthright, I don't figger that's any call for a celebration."

Arnie drew back as if he had been slapped. For a few minutes he had felt happy and free, but the bookkeeper, with his pickled face and snappish words, had succeeded in casting a pall over his youthful exuberance. He turned the cup up and emptied it, but the whisky had suddenly gone flat. Then he tramped through the store and stood for a while on the rear loading ramp, fuming helplessly.

Hefford, calmly puffing a cigar, came out and joined him. "Don't let Harve get under your hide, boy."

"He never had no right to talk to me like that. Birthright!"

The gun drummer sighed. "You got to look at it the way he does. This store's the same as a wife and family to Harve; it's hard for him to get it through his head that anybody could sell it."

"*I* can sell it! And that's just what I aim to do!"

"Gentle down, boy. Nobody's sayin' you can't. If it was mine I'd do the same thing. Nothin' but headaches and aggravations, runnin' a country store."

Arnie threw his arms wide in a gesture of helplessness. "I just don't understand him. He's hated my guts ever since I first landed here—you'd think he'd be *glad* to get rid of me and take on another partner."

The next day the freighter from the railhead arrived with the store's special order of Christmas goods. Arnie stood back amazed as the heavy wagon was unloaded at the rear ramp. Bags of shaggy coconuts were lugged to the front of the store and wedged in between block salt and hoe handles. Boxes of candy found room among the stores of coffee and sugar. Barrels of apples were opened and shoved up against the walls, along with crates of bright yellow oranges. Gaudy wood and metal toys were suspended from the ceiling along with the regular stock of water buckets, horse collars, buggy whips, lanterns, and lard cans. Small packages of violent red firecrackers, torpedoes, sparklers, and Roman candles were opened and displayed in their sawdust packing on the fancy goods counter. A tub of corned mackerel was placed alongside the pickle barrel and the crackers. A new supply of Maryland Bourbon and North Carolina corn whisky was crowded in alongside the regular stock.

Added to the everyday stock were extra supplies of pocketknives and cheap pistols and shotgun shells and Jew's harps and perfume. There was a dazzling array of exotic foodstuffs—great bunches of green and yellow bananas, boxes of nutmegs, lemon extract, raisins, mincemeat, chocolate, and citron and currants, and sticks of peppermint candy.

Arnie was shocked and appalled. "Has ever'body gone out of their head? What do you expect to do with all this stuff? Sodbusters can't afford this kind of fancy grub and doodads!"

Harve Purdy clamped his jaws and snapped, "Christmas time is special." He stood at the back door carefully checking off each box and barrel and sack and crate that entered the store.

The next morning Amy Hall took thick packages of green and red construction paper upstairs to the women's department and spent the whole day cutting and pasting together paper chains and Christmas bells. Arnie wandered about in a daze, in a store that he no longer recognized. Into every possible spare space someone had crammed in

215

some sort of exotic item that he was sure that nobody would ever buy, and if they did buy, could not pay for.

Even Robert Hefford seemed to be caught up in the madness. One entire day he helped Amy Hall string paper chains and hang the bright red Christmas bells. Harve Purdy, looking as grim and sour as ever, nevertheless deserted his books for half a day to help set up a display of toy dolls.

Arnie groaned, "I just hope ever'body comes to their right mind before Devero or somebody from the bank comes and sees how loco we are!"

Nobody paid any attention to him. By the end of the week the store was indeed something to see—even Arnie had to admit that much. And smell! A body could get lightheaded just standing in the doorway and breathing in the aroma of fresh fruits and spices and candies, all mingled with the acrid scents of coal oil and gunpowder and whisky, which somehow made it even more exciting.

A snapping, sputtering fire lazed in the giant black stove in the rear of the store. An occasional sodbuster would come in to gape at the new merchandise and warm himself by the post oak fire.

In the meantime Arnie's growing concern was mounting to the edge of panic. He cornered Purdy in his post office cubicle, which was now draped with a bright red and green Christmas chain. "Look here, what's goin' to happen if nobody buys all this crazy stuff? We'll be stuck with it, that's what!

How's that goin' to look on the books when the banker comes to buy the place?"

"I've been here forty Christmases," Purdy told him tartly. "We never got stuck."

"There's a first time for ever'thing. Just remember it's *me* that's tryin' to get the place off my hands, not you."

The bookkeeper looked at him over the top of his spectacles. "I remember."

A letter arrived from Herbert Webber in Placer. A man from the bank would be on hand to close the sale of the store, shortly after the first of the year. Arnie was instructed to have the books in order— and this did little to soothe his already frayed nerves. With so much new stock coming into the store, and Purdy spending less and less time on the books, it didn't seem possible that something wouldn't go wrong between now and the beginning of the new year.

A second freighter arrived from the railhead, this one loaded with more absolutely useless and worthless stock than he had ever seen at one time before. He watched in dismay as Hefford and the wagoner lugged in great barrels and boxes of glass bric-a-brac and fantastically decorated china. Stock was piled on top of stock and tumbled into the aisles. Arnie stared at a small mountain of gaudy plush-bound "memory books" that sentimental females would someday fill with photographs, locks of hair, scraps of cloth, pressed flowers, and

God knew what else. There was a fantastic litter of fancy glass bowls and vases and candy dishes. And a whole menagerie of colored glass animals that Arnie could not imagine a sodbuster buying, for whatever purpose, even if he had the money for such idiocies.

There was a fearful forest of coal oil lamps of all shapes and sizes, the chimneys gaudily painted or etched in every conceivable design, some of them equipped with the new flat "improved" wick, which hopefully would keep the lamp from exploding. There were dozens of fancy cups—mustache cups, shaving cups, tiny babies' cups aswarm with angels and roses. There were cheap comb and brush trays, manicure trays, hairpin and powderpuff boxes, and glass toothpick holders in every imaginable shape.

"Godamighty!" Arnie groaned to himself. "The store's ruined and I'm a blowed-up sucker!"

CHAPTER ELEVEN

Then came Saturday, two weeks before Christmas. Farm wagons labored over the half-frozen country roads bearing Christmas produce to be exchanged for credit at the store. The women brought baskets of eggs carefully packed in cottonseed. They brought butter in differing states of preservation. They came with tallow, and cottonseed, and shelled corn, and cowhides, and black walnuts and pecans.

Some of the wagons were loaded high with cord-wood, which the store would have to hold for almost a year when it would eventually be sold to the cotton gins in the fall. Children unloaded mountains of wild persimmons and nuts that they had been gathering since the first frost. The men carefully laid out their treasures of possum and coon and skunk hides for Harve Purdy to look at when he got the time.

Into a store that seemed already full to bursting the farm women came. They moved through the aisles in a mass, slowly, like a piston moving through a cylinder under pressure of steam. Longingly, they caressed china and glass atrocities while their husbands bargained with Harve Purdy over a temporary adjustment of credit.

Arnie grabbed Hefford at the lunch counter. "What are we goin' to do with all this produce? The sodbusters can't use it, they just brought it."

"Let Harve handle it; he knows what to do." The gun drummer finished dishing up a pint of fresh oysters into a small bucket. Fresh oysters! In the middle of the post oaks! They had been shipped all the way from New Orleans at a cost that Arnie didn't dare think about.

"I've concluded that Harve's out of his head! Either that, or he's out to ruin the store on purpose!"

"Draw yourself some bourbon," Hefford said quietly, as if he were gentling a young bronc just up from winter pasture. "Relax a little; it's Christmas time."

Arnie did not relax. He flitted nervously along the fringes of the activity, straining to understand the deals that Purdy was making for the produce. He watched the farmers unload their cordwood and methodically build a great post oak mountain behind the blacksmith shed. They stacked their hides on the rear loading ramp and arranged their cans of tallow in neat rows against the wall. They did it all with a certain precision, suggesting that they had done it many times before. Which they had.

By midafternoon the wagons began to rattle away from the hitching ground. By sundown the store was empty of customers but even more crowded with stock than it had been before. After all the hectic activity, the farmers had gone back home without buying any of Purdy's fancy merchandise.

"I'm ruined!" Arnie groaned to Robert Hefford, "I knowed them sodbusters wouldn't buy that stuff!"

"Take a drink of whisky," the gun drummer told him, busily scooping up some spilled coffee beans. "Better yet, get some fresh air. Hitch up my buggy and take Miss Amy home."

This had become a part of the Saturday routine. After the day's hectic activity was over he had come to look forward to the quiet ride to the Hall place, with Amy beside him. Sometimes he would stay for supper and later look at pictures of Niagara Falls though the Hall stereopticon. He knew what people were saying—that Amy Hall had set her hat for him. He didn't care what they said. Three weeks from now—with any kind of luck—he'd be hundreds of miles from here.

Hefford's gray mules plodded peacefully through the night. A pale moon shone high above the post oaks and there was a sleety taste in the air. Amy burrowed into her coat and shivered. "We don't usually get snow at Christmas time, but this year I think we will."

"That," Arnie said grimly, "is all I need. The roads blocked with snow. On top of Purdy doin' his best to ruin me."

"Mr. Purdy's all right," Amy said placidly. "When you get to know him."

I don't aim to be here that long, Arnie thought to himself. But he didn't say it. "Don't worry about the produce," Amy went on. "Every year the farmers bring it in this way—without it there wouldn't be any Christmas for most of them. You'll sell some of it to the stores in Placer. The rest you'll freight to the railhead and sell in Kansas City or somewhere."

"I wish I was as sure of it as you are."

"I'm sure because that's the way it always happens." The buggy lurched suddenly as the wheels slid into a rut, and for a moment they were in each other's arms. Amy smiled and asked, "Do you expect the time will ever come when we'll have decent roads in the post oaks?"

"I don't know." What's more, he didn't care.

"I expect they will. Sometime." They rode for a while in comfortable silence. Then Amy asked, "Have you ever been to a Christmas party in the country?"

"I've been to country dances and barn raisin's and things like that."

"There's a party at the schoolhouse on Christmas Eve." She said it absently, gazing up at the moon.

Arnie knew about the party. There had been post oak Christmas parties at one meeting house or another since before the Texas Revolution. He also knew that he was expected to be there this year, with Amy Hall on his arm.

She talked for some time about parties of the past. About fights and cutting scrapes, about love matches that had been made, about teams that had run away because of the fireworks. Arnie listened in silence. He knew that before Christmas Eve arrived he would ask Amy to go to the party with him, but there didn't seem to be any sense in rushing it.

For two days the store was almost deserted. Arnie prowled the crowded floors in panic. "I told Purdy nobody was goin' to buy this crazy stuff! Even a sodbuster's got more sense than that!"

"Gentle down," Robert Hefford told him calmly. "They got to think about it first. Christmas don't come but once a year; they don't want to use it up all at once."

Hefford loaded his buggy with produce that could be used locally—tallow, lard, homemade soap freshened with lavender, eggs, butter—and took it to the stores in Placer. The cowhides, the skins, the black walnuts and pecans, were loaded on a freighter, taken to the railhead, and from there they were shipped by train to dealers in St. Louis.

"How do you know anybody in St. Louis wants that stuff?" Arnie demanded.

"They'll want it," Purdy told him quietly. "They always do."

Another day passed, and the store was still empty of customers. Frantically, Arnie began composing a letter to Herbert Webber. Purdy had lost his mind. He had stocked the store with merchandise that nobody wanted. The situation was going downhill fast. Close the sale to Devero as soon as possible. If necessary, offer him a better bargain.

But in the end he tore up the letter. It was too late for that. Devero would take one look at this disastrously overstocked store and at Purdy's shady bookkeeping and throw the whole thing over.

Then Fred Medder's oldest boy arrived with an order for two coconuts, five pounds of apples, five pounds of oranges, a quarter pound of candied currants, one quart of Maryland whisky, and a medium bottle of morphine. Arnie was amazed that Purdy did not raise the roof when Hefford began getting the order together. Instead, he calmly recorded the transaction in his books and commented on the snappishness of the weather.

"A month ago," Arnie said indignantly, "Fred Medder's credit wasn't even good for five pounds of flour, now you're lettin' him have coconuts and apples and oranges and Lord knows what! Why didn't you throw in a half gallon of New Orleans oysters while you was at it?"

"The order never mentioned oysters," Purdy told him coolly. On the debit side of his book, Purdy recorded the items of the Medder purchase. On the credit side he set down ten gallons of tallow, four skunk hides, one cowhide, five dozen eggs, eight pounds of butter, and a bushel of black walnuts.

Arnie threw up his hands. "Hell's afire, this ain't no store, it's a goddamn Comanche tradin' post!"

Other orders for fancy foodstuffs began to arrive and, without argument, Purdy allowed them to be filled. Arnie stood helplessly by as hundreds of pounds of precious fruits and cheese and mackerel and herring were carried out of the store.

Then there was another day or so of quiet. The women were busy baking great white-frosted coconut cakes, and fruit cakes as heavy as cannon-balls and filled with rare currants and raisins, and figs from Egypt, and dates from Arabia. From their ovens rose the heady aroma of cooking wild turkey, possum, young squirrel, rabbit.

What the men were doing all this time, Arnie didn't know. Standing around gossiping, most likely, and drinking expensive Maryland Bourbon.

The day before Christmas Eve Arnie was disturbed by a new kind of activity. Sodbusters, looking as furtive as chicken thieves on a moonlit night, slunk about the store secretly conferring with Purdy and Amy Hall, or hovering about the stove chewing or smoking, with a faintly glassy look in their eyes. Then, almost before Arnie knew it, they were gone. And so was most of the stock in the store. They slipped out of the store as quietly as weasels in the dead of night, a Rochester lamp under one arm, a twenty-five-cent doll under the other, a package of firecrackers, a Roman candle.

Item by item of the gaudy goods of Purdy's special order was stripped from the shelves. Glass toothpick holders, tin-backed comb and brush sets, cheap mirrors in imitation ivory frames, hand-painted bud vases that would never see a flower. All the useless, idiotic trash that Arnie had long ago written off as a total loss—within two days it was all gone. The dozens of plush-bound memory books, the cheap perfume, the "Bohemian" glassware and china.

Arnie was stunned. By midday on Christmas Eve, all the "unsalable" merchandise had been sold. There was a catch, of course—none of the

225

stock had been paid for in cash, it had all been barter, but somehow Purdy in his mysterious way was even now balancing it up in his books. How it was going to look to the banker, Devero, Arnie didn't like to think about.

Amy Hall came down from the second floor. She heaved a sigh of relief and smiled at Arnie. "It's all over now. There won't be any more business today; everybody's home gettin' ready for Christmas mornin'. Or the party at the schoolhouse."

The party. The question of whether or not to take Amy to the party had been settled two days ago—he was taking her. Arnie suspected that there had never been any doubts in anybody's mind about it, least of all Amy's.

"Well," Arnie said, "there ain't much sense in stayin' on in an empty store." He hitched up Hefford's buggy and put on the isinglass side curtains and front windshield. The sky was clear; there was no sign of snow. The wind made a lonesome sound humming through the post oaks.

Riding beside him, Amy burrowed comfortably in her threadbare coat. She looked excited and happy. Arnie guessed that it didn't take much to make a sodbuster happy. Or a sodbuster's daughter.

"I got a feelin'," she said contentedly. "Next year's goin' to be better. More rain in the spring. Better crops. Patience is a virtue; it says that in the Bible. Folks hereabouts have got plenty of patience."

Folks hereabouts have also got overdue mortgages and debts that they can't begin to pay, Arnie thought to himself.

Amy wiped the mist from the isinglass. A kind of smoky haze had settled over the thickets of scrub timber—it was easy to see that Amy thought it was beautiful. Most likely it was the only country she had ever seen.

Give me the prairie every time, Arnie thought silently. He longed to hear the bawling of cattle again. He was sick of the sound of wind moaning through the post oaks. Still, he had to admit that it was pleasant enough sitting here beside a pretty girl, riding across a smoky countryside with the unseen excitement of Christmas in the air.

"The party won't start till late," Amy said as Arnie swung the buggy into the Hall dooryard. "Seven o'clock, most likely."

"That's all right," Arnie said. "There's some things at the store I've got to see to."

Andrew Hall came out and greeted Arnie with a conspiratorial wink and a bourbon breath. "If you was to come out to the barn a minute," he whispered from the side of his mouth, "it might be I could introduce you to an old friend."

Arnie knew all about that friend. The one from Maryland that Hall still owed the store for. But he only said, "Maybe when I come back later. I got some things at the store to see to."

"Later then. Happy Christmas to you."

"Happy Christmas." Arnie turned the buggy around and headed back to the store.

Robert Hefford was sitting next to the bourbon barrel with a cup of whisky in his hand. He saluted Arnie gravely as he came through the back door. "Happy Christmas, storekeeper."

Arnie grinned. "Same to you. Looks like you're gettin' an early start."

"I like to do my drinkin' when Purdy ain't here to watch every drop that comes out of the barrel. But don't worry. I keep track."

"I ain't worried." Arnie wandered about the store, as a matter of habit, seeing that the dry goods tables were covered and everything was in place. For one reckless moment he considered heating some water and giving himself an allover bath, but quickly decided that a clean shirt and a new union suit and plenty of bay rum would do just as well. He returned to the bourbon barrel, drew himself a small dram, and downed it. For several minutes he stood gazing blankly into space.

"She's a pretty gal, all right," Hefford said with a crooked smile.

Arnie blinked. "What're you talkin' about?"

"Miss Amy, of course."

"I wasn't thinkin' about her. I was thinkin' about the rollin' grassland down along the Brazos. Cow country. That's where I'll be, about two weeks from now."

Hefford looked at him steadily for several seconds. Then he drained his cup and said with bleak politeness, "Boy, I've just made up my mind about you. I've decided you're a fool."

CHAPTER TWELVE

In the cramped sleeping room Arnie changed shirts and underwear and doused himself with bay rum. He was ready for the party.

Hefford was still in the store, in the same place beside the bourbon barrel. A lone lantern sputtered above the meat box. The room was full of shadows and ghosts; they were old friends of Hefford's.

Over there next to the fancy goods counter was Abby Capps. Abby was young and fair and reckless—he would have been twenty-five this Christmas, if Hefford hadn't killed him. Chances were that he wouldn't have amounted to much. He had been loudmouthed, cocky, and he had been obsessed with the notion that he could outdraw Robert Wakefield Hefford. He had been wrong. Now he was dead, and it didn't matter much what he *might* have been.

There sitting on the dry goods counter, his long legs dangling, a bitter grin on his unhandsome face, was Albert Trott. Albert had, for reasons best known to himself, hated all lawmen and never passed up a chance to kill one, if he thought it could be done with complete safety to himself. His mistake had been in thinking that, because Hefford's eyes were closed and his breathing slow and measured, he was sleeping. That mistake had been a fatal one for Albert Trott.

And Mose Carson, mild-mannered, soft spoken—and deadly. Mose had murdered his Indian wife and ran off with her allotment money. He had been lucky—instead of hanging on the gallows at Fort Smith, Hefford had given him peace with a single bullet through the heart. Probably Mose had not appreciated that kindness. Mose Carson had not been an appreciative man.

Over by the lunch counter was a ghostly shape that Hefford could not quite make out. Maybe it was Joe Hardy, the Chickasaw murderer that he had run down and killed in the Winding Stairway Mountains. Or Richie Malloy, whose crimes were so black that they were not even talked about in polite society.

Hefford raised his cup and saluted. "Whoever you are. Happy Christmas to you." Lord, he thought bleakly, I feel a hundred years old. And I must be as crazy as a Comanche *pukutsi*, settin' here in the dark talkin' to the ghosts of men I've killed.

Arnie came in the back way, freshly shaved, his hair plastered slickly to his skull, reeking of bay rum. "Ain't you ready for the party yet?"

Hefford shrugged. "Christmas is for the young'uns. I don't feel that young tonight."

"Didn't I hear you talkin' to somebody?"

The gun drummer smiled. "That was Richie Malloy."

Arnie didn't ask who Richie Malloy was; he had seen Hefford like this before. "I'm takin' your buggy to ride Amy to the schoolhouse if that's all right with you."

"It's all right with me." When Arnie started to leave, Hefford straightened up and asked, "Ain't you forgettin' somethin'?"

"What's that?"

"When I was a young sprout takin' girls to Christmas play parties it was considered the gentlemanly thing to take along a present."

Arnie slapped himself on the forehead. "I clean forgot! What am I goin' to do? The store's cleaned out of all the fancy falderal."

Hefford heaved himself to his feet and took a package from beneath the fancy goods counter. It was a small parcel neatly wrapped in red crepe paper and tied with a green ribbon. Arnie looked at it suspiciously. "What is it?"

"A bottle of Hoyt's cologne. I figgered you'd forget."

"Cologne? Ain't that kind of . . . personal?"

"Of course it's personal. What do you think a girl expects from a gent that's been sashayin' her around the county every Sunday for six months?"

"Well . . ." It wasn't as if he had a choice. He took the package gingerly and dropped it in his coat pocket. "Happy Christmas, Hefford."

"Happy Christmas, boy." He went back to his seat next to the whisky barrel and refilled his cup.

There were perhaps twenty rigs of various kinds pulled up on the hitching ground in front of the schoolhouse, and several saddle animals were standing at the rack on the south side of the building. Arnie, feeling awkward and out of place in the midst of so many sodbusters, greeted several store customers who were standing around the schoolyard, chewing, smoking, gossiping, just as they did every Saturday at the store.

Arnie looked at Amy, and she laughed, knowing what he was thinking. A gentle wind, mild for December, carried the spicy fragrance of Maryland Bourbon across the schoolyard. Next spring, Arnie thought, they'll be wantin' more credit for grub, and I'll remind them about this whisky. He had forgotten for the moment that he would not be here in the spring.

Amy was looking at him again in that knowing way she had. "It's only once a year," she said. "When times are hard, it seems that the post oaks don't come alive except for a little while at Christmas time."

Arnie scowled. "I didn't say anything." They walked across the schoolyard to the building where Matt Loving, in his role as preacher and leading citizen, greeted them. The interior of the school building had been cleared out, except for a big cedar Christmas tree and a few benches reserved for old folks and nursing mothers. The single large room was crowded with women and children. The children were whooping and chasing one another about the room while the women carried on with their eternal gossiping.

Arnie shifted from one foot to the other, not knowing what to do with himself. At the rear of the room there was a table that sagged dangerously under the weight of dozens of cakes, mountains of fried chicken and squirrel and rabbit, and buckets of hot coffee. No wonder they don't have enough to eat all the rest of the year, Arnie thought to himself. But he didn't say it.

"Look at the children," Amy said. "How lively they are."

"They're lively, all right. And loud." He began to look for a way to get out.

Amy laughed. "Go outdoors, if you want to. Most of the men will be out there until the children's program is over."

With relief, Arnie edged his way toward the door. Matt Loving stopped him for a moment. "Was there somethin' you wanted to leave at the tree?" the former clerk said delicately.

"What?"

"A present for Miss Amy. You brought one, didn't you?"

"Oh, yes." He dug the package out of his pocket and handed it to Loving. "I ain't quite got the hang of these country parties. I'd be much obliged if you put this on the tree for me."

He escaped the chattering, whooping swirl of women and children and moved quickly into the cool darkness outside the schoolhouse. What I ought to of done, he thought to himself, is to stay at the store with Hefford. At least he's somebody I could talk to, not like a bunch of sodbusters.

Somebody pressed a flat whisky bottle in his hand. "Happy Christmas, Mr. Smith."

"Happy Christmas to you." He wasn't sure who the man was. As Arnie had noted several times before, after a while all sodbusters began to look alike. He turned the bottle up and took a long swallow. Don't think this is goin' to get you more credit next spring, he thought, as he returned the bottle. Because I won't be here then.

Wandering about the schoolyard, Arnie had several more whisky bottles pressed into his hand. "Happy Christmas, Mr. Smith."

"Happy Christmas to you."

After a while a quiet, cheerful stupor took hold of him. He stood for minutes at a time grinning blankly while sodbusters told him pointless stories about politicians, or preachers, or other sodbusters. Finally a group of children, led by Amy Hall, began singing "Silent Night" and some of the younger married men went inside to be with their families. Arnie stayed outside with the others. Bottles passed from hand to hand. Arnie moved to one of the schoolhouse windows and watched the proceedings inside.

There was a pageant of some sort involving several small bed-sheet angels. Arnie didn't understand it, but apparently the sodbusters did. Then there was some singing and a short talk by Matt Loving. Finally a lanky sodbuster, padded with down pillows and rigged out in a red-dyed muslin Santa Claus suit, lunged drunkenly through the back door, and all the children squealed.

A man handed Arnie a bottle and he took a short drink. "I heard country parties was famous for their dancin' and hell raisin'," he said. "All I seen so far tonight is women and young'uns."

"Dancin' comes later," the man told him. "After all the presents get handed out."

Loving and Santa Claus and Amy Hall distributed oranges and apples and hard candy to the children—other presents, if there were to be others, would come later, at home. Finally the children were herded to one corner of the room to chatter excitedly among themselves. There was a good deal of nervous giggling and blushing among the younger couples as Santa Claus prepared to hand out the presents.

Arnie was beginning to be bored by it all. "Miss Amy Hall!" Santa Claus hollered, and there was a murmur of approval and even a little hand clapping as Amy accepted the small red-wrapped package.

A strong, lean hand took hold of Arnie's arm, and

he turned and looked into the face of Matt Loving. "Don't you think you ought to be indoors with Miss Amy?"

"Why? Most of the men are out here."

"Old married men, or ones that don't never aim to get married." With surprising strength, Matt guided him through the crowd of sodbusters and in the doorway. "Mr. Arnie Smith," Santa Claus bellowed as Loving brought Arnie to a halt next to Amy Hall.

Arnie accepted a small parcel wrapped in green crepe paper. From its shape and size he knew what it was—an imitation ivory-backed hairbrush. He had seen Purdy sell it to Amy two days before. Everybody was looking at him, waiting to see what he would do. Arnie waved the package over his head, as if it had been a prize he had won roping calves. It seemed to be the right thing; everybody laughed.

Amy was saying, "It's a beautiful bottle of cologne. Just what I wanted."

Arnie shifted feet and ran a finger around the collar of his hickory shirt. "Much obliged," he said, "for the hairbrush."

"You haven't opened it yet, how do you know it's a hairbrush?"

Santa Claus hollered, "Mr. Arnie Smith?"

To a round of good-humored clapping, Arnie accepted a second package. This one was about a foot square, was moderately heavy, and rattled dryly. Arnie looked at Amy Hall in amazement. "Black walnuts! What fool would be givin' me black walnuts? I got a store full of them."

"Shhh!" Amy said sternly. "Try to look pleased!"

Arnie grinned crookedly, held up the box and waved to the laughing crowd. "Who's it from? There ain't any writin' on the box."

"Maybe it's in the box," Amy told him. "Maybe there ain't any. Maybe somebody just wanted to give you a present, and walnuts is all he had."

Arnie didn't understand it and he wasn't sure that he liked it. He stood there, sweating lightly and feeling silly, with the box of nuts under his arm. He hoped the name calling would soon be over and the dancing would get started.

"Mr. Arnie Smith!" Santa Claus bellowed for the third time.

Dazed, Arnie accepted a hand-plaited horsehair belt wrapped in plain white paper. "What's goin' on here? This one ain't got a name on it, either."

"Act pleased!" Amy hissed under her breath.

Sweating freely now, Arnie grinned and nodded to the crowd. Worriedly, he nudged Amy with his elbow. "Do you know what's goin' on here?"

"I think so."

"Then tell me! I don't like to be made a fool of and not even know what the hoorahin's about!"

"They're not hoorahin'," Amy said quietly. "They're thankin' you for the things you've done.

And they're tellin' you they don't want to see you leave the post oaks."

Arnie stared at her. Before Amy could say anything, Santa Claus was bellowing again, "Mr. Arnie Smith!"

"Listen here!" Arnie said angrily from the side of his mouth. "I want to know what these sodbusters are up to!"

"Their children," Amy said with a sigh. "The cod liver oil. The vegetable seed. The times you made Purdy extend their credit when you knew they were already in over their heads. They want to say 'thank you' and this is the only way they know."

Arnie almost wished she hadn't told him. Instead of being angry, he was now embarrassed. Every time the scrawny, cotton-bearded Santa Claus yelled, "Mr. Arnie Smith!" his stomach curled.

By the time the name calling was over he had accumulated a dozen or more presents of varying shapes and sizes. Most of them, he knew without looking, were as thoroughly worthless as the walnuts. "I think I better go," he said to Amy. "What I need is a drink."

"You've had enough," she told him, smiling brightly.

A fiddler struck up "Buffalo Girls." Half of the crowd headed for the lunch table, the other half formed a circle in the middle of the room. "All join hands!" the caller yelled. The main part of the party was underway.

To Arnie's immense relief, dancing in the post oaks was the same as cow country dancing. The uninhibited couples whooped and stomped, more or less in time to the music, raising a great noise and a choking cloud of dust.

"How often do you have parties like this?" Arnie hollered, as the musicians swung into "Black and White Rag."

"Pretty often," Amy hollered back. "When times are good."

After a while they took a breather and went to the lunch table where Arnie ate a chicken leg and three pieces of coconut cake and drank a cup of bitter black coffee. "You want to know where I was this time last year?" Arnie asked.

Amy looked at him "Where?"

"In a line shack, down by the Big Sandy River. Me and a family of coyotes and a settlement of prairie dogs. I had sowbelly for supper and then rode out to pull one of the boss's cows out of a bog."

She laughed. "It must be a lonesome life, bein' a cowhand."

"I didn't think much about it then." He thought about it now, for a few seconds. He had to admit that this was a better way to spend Christmas Eve. Even if it was among sodbusters.

The music started again and the dancers began forming their circle. A white-faced sodbuster, got up in a shapeless jean suit, suddenly appeared in the doorway and started to holler.

At first no one paid any attention to him. There was a great deal of noise. The music, the laughter, the hand clapping, the dancing. "The store's on fire!" the man yelled. Then they heard him.

The dancers froze. The fiddlers' tune trailed off into silence. Matt Loving stepped forward and, in his quiet way, asked, "What did you say, Henry?"

"The store's on fire! Me and Ruth was late comin' to the party, on account of a sick cow. As we was comin' along the section line road, we seen it. You can see it outdoors now."

The crowd moved in a mass toward the door. Dumbly, Arnie found himself being moved, through no effort of his own, out the door and into the schoolyard. A long, aching sigh went up as they saw it. An unmistakable pink glow tinted the northern sky. It had to be the store. There was nothing else in that particular place.

Arnie felt a sinking sensation in the pit of his stomach. He looked around for Amy. "I better go see how bad it is."

"I'll go with you."

Within a matter of minutes most of the rigs were off the schoolground and on the deep-rutted road, racing north. Arnie did not try to anticipate what he would find. His mind was curiously blank as Hefford's mules strained forward in their harness. Amy sat beside him on the leather seat, her hands in her lap. From the time they left the schoolhouse to the time they reached the store grounds, they did not speak.

The store building was in fiery ashes by the time they got there. Sodbusters from the few rigs that had got there ahead of them were milling about the grounds. "Has anybody seen Hefford?" Arnie hollered. "He was in the store when I left."

A farmer came out of the flame-painted night. "Hefford's over there." He pointed. "He's hurt bad. I wouldn't try to move him just now."

Arnie turned the buggy lines over to Amy Hall and raced across the store yard. Hefford was lying in some weeds, beyond the hackberry tree. His face looked curiously white and drawn in the firelight, but he managed a grin as Arnie knelt beside him.

"Hold on, Hefford," Arnie told him. "I'll send somebody to Placer for Doc McPhitter."

"McPhitter." Hefford smiled. "Never mind. There ain't time for that, anyhow. Is Purdy here?"

"I saw him at the schoolhouse. He's here some-wheres."

Hefford made a small gesture with one hand. "Get him."

Somebody went after Purdy. Arnie felt cold and empty and helpless. Hefford's chest was stiff with dried blood. He had been lying there for what must have been a long time, his life slowly bleeding away. Arnie knew instinctively that neither McPhitter nor any other doctor could help him.

"Do you feel like talkin', Hefford? Can you tell me what happened?"

The gun drummer sighed, almost as if the subject bored him. "The scavengers came back. I figgered they would. Frank Carr's dead, over there in the weeds somewheres. And one of his boys. The rest of them lit out—I don't figger you'll be seein' more of them." He lay still for a minute, breathing very shallowly and carefully. "I'm sorry about the store. They set fire to it before I knowed they was here."

"It's all right about the store. I was never any storekeeper anyhow."

A grim-faced Harve Purdy, trailed by several farmers, tramped across the store yard and stopped in front of Hefford.

The gun drummer looked at him with glassy eyes. "I saved your books, Harve. And most of the files, I think. That's all the time I had before the buildin' went up."

In amazement, Purdy knelt down and lightly fingered the heavy books at Hefford's side. Then he quickly inspected his goods box files. "Yes," he said quietly. "Everythin's here."

One of the farm women brought a wool lap robe from a buggy and spread it over Hefford. Somebody said, "Jim's gone after Doc McPhitter."

A sodbuster handed Harve Purdy a bottle of whisky. Arnie was shocked to see the bookkeeper turn the bottle up and take three big gulps without batting an eye.

• • •

Hefford died about two hours before sunup. The women had brought up some burning planks and kept a small fire going beside him. But he died. There ain't even a coffin to bury him in, Arnie thought bleakly. The factory-made coffins had burned with the store. Even the brass coffin fittings were burned or lost in the smoking rubble.

Matt Loving knelt down beside the gun drummer and closed his eyes. "Rest in peace, Hefford. I reckon you've earned that."

Arnie walked away from the stunned crowd. He stood for a long while in the darkness, by himself, a great rage burning inside him. Hefford was the only man in the whole region who had been willing to be Arnie Smith's friend, no questions asked. Now he was dead. All because of a country store that Arnie had never really wanted in the first place.

He was savagely furious that Frank Carr was dead, because he wanted so much to kill him himself. But there was not even that satisfaction to be had now. These goddamn post oaks! he thought bitterly. Everything a body touches here turns to rot.

After a while Amy Hall came up to him and said, "Arnie, I know the way you felt about Hefford. But there's nothin' to be done now. Matt Lovin' and some of the others are makin' arrangements for the buryin'. Have you thought about where you're goin' to sleep?"

He hadn't thought about sleeping at all. He looked

243

at her blankly. "You can stay in the barn loft at our place, if you want to," she said, "until you're more settled in your mind, anyhow. It's tight and warm."

"I'll think about it," he said. He walked away from her and went to where two bodies were stretched out on the ground a respectable distance from Hefford: Frank Carr and one of his scavengers.

A smoky dawn began to show through the timber. Arnie discovered that a light coat of frost had settled on his shoulders and he was chilled to the bone. One by one, the farm families began to leave. Croy Mackerson and some neighbors took Hefford's body with them; they would make a coffin themselves out of old goods boxes and scrap lumber. Somebody else took the scavengers.

By the harsh light of dawn the store grounds looked like a field where some savage battle had been fought. Only the rock foundation remained; all the rest was charred and smoking embers. This was what Syrus Smith had worked a lifetime for. What Robert Wakefield Hefford died for. All in all, it seemed to Arnie that it had been a poor bargain.

By midmorning almost everybody had gone home. Only Arnie and Purdy and Matt Loving remained. The farmer who had gone to Placer for Doc McPhitter returned shortly before noon. "I'm sorry, Mr. Purdy," he said to the bookkeeper. "Doc McPhitter couldn't come hisself. But he sent a bottle of morphine."

Purdy took the bottle of morphine from him and

244

said dryly, "I'll save it for Delly Medder. She'll be needin' it before long." The bookkeeper stared hard-eyed at the ruins of the store building. More than half of his life was mingled in that rubble of smoking ashes. "It's a hard thing," he said at last. "But at least we've got the books and records. Thanks to Hefford."

Suddenly all of Arnie's rage rushed into his throat. "What the hell difference does it make? There ain't any store!"

"A store," Purdy told him flatly, "is more than a building and stock on the shelves."

They buried Hefford the next afternoon in the Oak College Cemetery, on a section line road south of the schoolhouse. Matt Loving preached a short funeral in the schoolhouse, and some of the farm women sang "Bread of Life" and then they loaded the new coffin into Mackerson's wagon and took it to the graveyard.

Arnie looked around at all the faces that he had seen just the night before at the party. They looked tired. Most of them hadn't had any more sleep than he had—the men who had built the coffin hadn't slept at all. The cedar Christmas tree had been removed from the big room, but Christmas chains and paper bells and sprigs of mistletoe were still decorating the windows and doorway.

" 'Beyond the sacred page I seek Thee, Lord,' " the sodbuster ladies sang, " 'my spirit pants for

Thee, O living Word!'" And the men lowered Robert Wakefield Hefford into the ground. There alongside Texans who had fought with Bowie and Houston. Maybe Hefford would like that.

When or where the two scavengers were buried, Arnie never heard.

Amy Hall came up beside him as he was walking away from the cemetery. "I know it seems hard now," she said. "But give it time, Arnie. It will get better."

"Maybe," he said flatly, "but I won't be here to see it."

She looked at him, her heart filled with passionate arguments to keep him here. But she only said, "Where did you sleep last night? Pa had a place fixed for you in the barn."

"I went home with Purdy and his brother's family. Purdy wanted to go over the books with me." Lord, he thought to himself, I feel as old as these Texas hills! His stomach was sour, his mouth cottony. This is the end of the line, he thought. I landed here with nothin', and I'm leavin' with nothin'! But at that, I'm luckier than Hefford.

He shook hands with several farmers as they drifted away from the cemetery. Most of them he never expected to see again.

When they reached the road, where Hefford's buggy was standing, Amy smiled faintly and gave Arnie her hand. "Will you be goin' soon?"

"As soon as I get things straight with Purdy."

"Will I be seein' you again?"

"Sure," he said, knowing that she wouldn't.

Purdy and Arnie rode back together in Hefford's heavy two-horse buggy. The bookkeeper looked at Arnie over the steel rims of his spectacles. "You feel like talkin' business?"

Arnie nodded, although he didn't know what there was left to talk about. The store was gone.

"I sent Patty Doul to Placer to get Herbert Webber to get the banker Devero. He'll be here in two, three days, if I'm any judge of bankers. And you can wind up the sale—if you still want to go through with it."

"Is there anything left to sell?"

Purdy settled back with the air of a man who has some tedious explaining to do. "I told you before, there's more to a store than just a buildin' and the stock in it. The biggest part of it is tied up in liens and mortgages, in cotton and land. That's what the bank is interested in buyin'. Not the buildin'." He flipped his hand in a curious gesture of dismissal. "The bank will never build back the store, of course."

Arnie looked at him sharply. "Why won't they?"

"Because banks ain't in the store business; they're in the land and cotton business."

"What will happen to your interest if they don't rebuild?"

Purdy allowed himself one of his rare smiles. "I guess I'll go into the bankin' business."

Arnie thought about that for a while. "What about the farmers?"

"Well? What about them?"

"If they fall behind in their payments, will the bank foreclose on them?"

"Like I said, land is the bank's business. And the way to get land at bargain prices is to foreclose on late debts."

Something in Arnie seemed to sag. He had had his share of trouble with sodbusters, but he had come to understand them too.

For three days Arnie stayed with Harve at Whit Purdy's farm. He slept in the barn loft and ate with the family, and in between he helped mend harness and repair equipment and scrape rusty tools. This was the sort of thing that farmers did during the winter months. Arnie had always thought that from December to April a sodbuster didn't do anything but lay around and spin yarns.

On the fourth day Patty Doul brought Arnie some mail for the store. "Where did you get this?" Arnie asked. "The post office went up in fire."

"Yes, sir," the young clerk said. "But I've been takin' it at the schoolhouse and passin' it out to folks that come by."

"I ain't sure the government's goin' to like that."

"The way I look at it," Doul said, "is what the government don't know won't hurt it. I didn't want word to get back to Washington that we was out of a post office here—they might move it some-wheres else."

Arnie scowled. "They're bound to find out sooner or later."

"I reckon. But I figgered if we could keep it from them till the store was built back . . ."

Arnie had run into this before—the refusal, or inability, of the sodbuster to believe that the store would not be rebuilt. "All right, Patty, thanks for bringin' it out." He leafed through the letters and found one from Herbert Webber. He read it and looked at Purdy. "You was right about bankers. Devero will be here tomorrow with all the papers. Patty, does the stage still stop at the store grounds?"

"Yes sir."

"Brush up your jeans suit, Harve. You're about to go into the bankin' business."

They arrived at the store grounds well ahead of stage time, though Arnie knew from experience that the coach was almost always an hour late. He made a sound of amazement when he saw what was happening. "Harve, what's goin' on here? What's them fools think they're doin'?"

If Purdy was amazed, or even mildly surprised, there was nothing in his long face to show it. "Looks to me like they're settin' the frame to build another store."

There were perhaps a dozen wagons on the

grounds and two dozen farmers hammering and sawing and planing green rawhide lumber. Part of a frame was already up, laid on the rock foundation which was still standing. The few things that the fire hadn't ruined completely—the big iron stove and a few granite utensils—had been moved out of the way and covered with a ragged tarpaulin. The burned rubble had been removed and the ground scraped clean.

Arnie went up to Aram Plott, who was laboriously measuring an angle for jointing. "Aram, what the hell do you think you're doin' here?"

The big farmer looked at him soberly. "Why, fixin' a joint to frame the window on the right side of the door, Mr. Smith."

Arnie moved on to where a group of men was setting the back door frame. "Croy," he said patiently to Croy Mackerson, "I appreciate what you and the others are doin', but it ain't any use. The store's done for; I'm sellin' out."

Croy Mackerson nodded gravely. "Yes, sir, that's what we heard."

"Then why are you wastin' your time here. Why are you doin' this?"

The farmer shrugged. "Well, there's always been a store here, as far back as anybody can recollect. It don't seem right not to have one."

"Croy, I'm sellin' out to a bank. The bank don't want a store. All this work is for nothin'."

"Yes, sir," Croy agreed sorrowfully, "that's what

they say." Then he went back to setting the frame.

The yellow store cat came strolling across the grounds and rubbed against Arnie's legs. Arnie picked him up and scratched his ears. "How you doin', son? I was beginnin' to figger we'd lost you in the fire." He prodded the animal's gaunt ribs with his finger. "Hard times for cats as well as people, looks like. No more sardines. No more salmon or cove oysters. Well, you'll soon learn to rustle for yourself."

He put the cat down and made a slow circle of the workers, trying to explain to them that all their trouble was going for nothing. They would nod and agree and perhaps grin sheepishly, and then they would go on doing what they had been doing before.

Fred Medder said, "The lumber ain't cured. When it starts to dry out there's goin' to be some warpin'. But we can chink it some to keep out the wind."

"Fred, I won't be able to use it. I'm sellin' out."

Medder stepped back a few paces and looked with pride at a joint that he had just made. "It won't be like the old place, of course. But she'll last a year or so, till you can put up somethin' better."

Arnie sighed in resignation and went back to Purdy. "Ain't there any way I can make them understand?"

"They understand. In their heads, they do. But a sodbuster lives by the growlin' in his guts, not what's in his head." He turned and looked to the south. "Here comes the stage. It's on time for once."

The coach drew up on the hitching ground in a great cloud of dust. The driver waved and hollered to Arnie. "Buildin' back again, are you? Glad to see it!"

Arnie didn't have the heart to try to explain; he merely waved. "Left the mail at the schoolhouse with young Doul," the driver told him. He studied the activity with growing interest, then, with a shrug, he wrapped his lines and climbed down for a closer look. It didn't matter if the stage was a little late.

Devero climbed out of the coach and came toward Purdy and Arnie, leaving behind him a fragrant trail of good tobacco and lavender cologne. He glanced sternly toward the construction activity. "What's the meaning of this, Mr. Smith? I understood from Mr. Webber that you were not rebuilding."

"I'm not. It's their idea."

"Haven't you told them the business is changing hands and the store won't be rebuilt?"

"I told them. But with some folks it takes a while."

Mr. Devero frowned in mild disapproval. "Well, I don't suppose it matters." He opened a cowhide case and took out two sets of papers. He handed one set to Arnie, the other to Purdy. "Terms of the sale have been agreed to by your lawyer in Placer, Mr. Webber. All that is needed is your signature witnessed and sealed by a notary public. Mr. Purdy, you are a notary public, I believe?"

Harve Purdy nodded absently, reading his copy of the agreement carefully, word by word. Arnie looked at his copy but did not read it.

If Purdy said it was all right, it was all right. He would sign it and get his money, and he would leave these post oaks forever.

Purdy read to the last word and folded his papers. "Considerin' the money panic, it seems like a fair offer," he said to Arnie.

Good-by forever to these damned post oaks, Arnie was thinking. And yet, he would be leaving a great deal of himself here. More than he had ever left anywhere else. "There ain't any pen or ink," he heard himself saying.

Devero waved away that small difficulty. "I have an indelible pencil; that will do just as well."

He held out the pencil, but Arnie only looked blankly past him to the scrub thickets beyond the burned-out store. A friend was buried there. And so was another Smith.

The banker said with flagging patience, "Mr. Smith, I had hoped to continue on with this coach and make my Fort Worth connections this afternoon. But first the sale agreements must be signed."

Over there, Arnie was thinking, is where that

bunch of sodbusters hauled me down from the porch and stomped me. Six months later they're givin' me Christmas presents and rebuildin' the store. There ain't a man amongst the whole bunch of them that's got the sense of a muley cow. I ain't seen one yet that's fit even to wrangle horses, let alone tend cattle. A man would have to be out of his head to live amongst such people.

"Mr. Smith?" Devero was looking vaguely disturbed. "Is anything the matter?"

"Maybe. But I ain't sure just what it is."

"Will you please sign on this line, Mr. Smith. The coach will be leaving any minute now."

Before he came to the post oaks nobody had ever called him Mister. Amy Hall's face flashed in his mind. And two dozen ripe persimmons touched by the first frost. He didn't even like persimmons. But then nobody had ever given him any before, either.

He took a deep breath and looked at Purdy and sighed. "Harve, if the store was rebuilt, could we make a go of it? Could we get enough credit from the suppliers to keep us goin' till times got better?"

Purdy shrugged. He did not seem particularly surprised by the sudden question. "Maybe. I've been doin' business with some of the companies for a long while."

Mr. Devero's face had gone from pink to warm red to beet red. "Look here, Mr. Smith, it's too late, much too late . . . !"

Arnie handed him back the papers. "I'm sorry

about puttin' you to all this trouble, Mr. Devero, but I guess I won't be sellin', after all."

The banker bit his teeth together until the muscles in his jaws jumped like frogs. "Very well, Mr. Smith! The decision is yours; I hope you won't regret it!"

"Me, too. I sure do hope that."

For a moment they were all aware of the sudden silence. Even the stage team seemed to stand motionless. The yellow cat sat on the ground and looked up at Arnie without moving. The farmer-carpenters stood in frozen little groups, watching.

Then Devero turned and got into the coach. The driver climbed over the wheel to the box, and the stage exploded out of the store yard in boiling dust. There it goes, Arnie thought with a curious absence of emotion, maybe the only chance I'll ever have to get away from here.

Behind him, the sodbusters took up their sawing and hammering with renewed vigor.

Center Point Publishing

600 Brooks Road ● PO Box 1
Thorndike ME 04986-0001 USA

(207) 568-3717

US & Canada:
1 800 929-9108

www.centerpointlargeprint.com